ALWAYS A BIGGER FISH

Arlie Undercover, Book 3

Dani Haviland

USA Today Bestselling Author

Always a Bigger Fish and the *Arlie Undercover* series are works of fiction. Names, place, characters, and incidents are the product of the author's imagination and are used for the readers' enjoyment. Any resemblance to persons living, dead, or fictional, events or business establishments is entirely coincidental.

Book Description

Detective Arlie Bigger is hoping for a boring caseload after recovering from a stabbing wound that nearly took his life, but an intimidating package has just arrived at the forensics department. It seems that someone is out to take his and his US Deputy Marshal buddy's scalps.

Acknowledgment

Thanks to all who serve, whether as a paid occupation, a volunteer, or just as a random act of kindness. We all need each other at one time or another, so share yourself!

Chapter 1
Job Opportunities

Though completion of an Alaska paralegal program is not required by law, it is a competitive career move. Voluntary certification through a national paralegal association such as the National Association of Legal Assistants (NALA) or the National Federation of Paralegal Associations (NFPA) is also recommended. Certification through these organizations carries prerequisite education and/or work experience requirements and although national certification is not required by most states, it is a valuable credential.
https://www.paralegal411.org/careers/alaska/

"I really didn't think you'd recover from your injuries so quickly," Charlene said dreamily, then looked at her exhausted newlywed husband, lying flat on his back beside her, his bare chest glistening in the glow of the LED nightlight. "Maybe those vitamins helped."

A satisfied groan rumbled through Arlie as he turned his neck to face her, too spent to move the rest of his body. "I'd rather believe it was the proper motivation. It's been a while since... I mean... Shoot, I can't remember..." *Shut up, dude! She doesn't need to know about how long it's been since you've been with a woman or anything else about your prior relationships!*

"I've never had any experience in my life—past or present—as wonderful as making love to you," Arlie said, and squeezed her hand as a tacit apology.

A giggle escaped Charlene. "Nice save, dear. We both have a past. I'm sure neither of us cares to hear about old flames or foibles, but you're right. It's the partner involved that makes it fantastic, right."

"Uh huh!"

"If you don't mind, I think I'll roll over and catch another few winks before the alarm goes off and I have to get the boys ready for school," Charlene said, then nuzzled her face into her pillow.

"I can handle them, if you'd like. I really don't feel sleepy at all anymore. I spent enough time on my back in the hospital. I mean, you got my heart and lungs up and running and I'm rarin' to go," Arlie said, then leaned over and kissed the back of her neck.

"Oh, no, you don't," she replied, then reached back to find

him. "Lie back down and save your strength. After the boys are off to school, I might want some more one-on-one time."

Knock, knock, knock!

"Mommy! Daddy! Is it time for school yet?" Chip asked. "Carlos said it was too early, but I know that it's still dark in the mornings in Alaska."

"Yeah, but the clock says it's only six o'clock," Carlos added.

"I'll be right there, boys," Arlie said, then turned back to Charlene. "You take a few more minutes. I'll keep them entertained for a bit. I promise, I won't wear myself out."

"Okay," Charlene said. "I'm sure glad Chip has a dad now. Being a single parent was such a time thief." She grabbed Arlie's pillow and put it over her head and mumbled, "Thanks," and was out before he had his pants on.

"All right, boys. What do you want for breakfast? Bacon, eggs, pancakes? Nah, just kidding. We have cereal, fruit, and toaster waffles."

"I want some of that colored circles cereal," Chip said.

Arlie scanned the cupboards and double checked the pantry. "Nope. No boxed cereal. Looks like Mom is on a health kick." Arlie opened the refrigerator and freezer. "Well, I guess I was wrong. Looks like I either have to make oatmeal or maybe some pancakes from scratch."

"Pancakes, pancakes," the boys chanted.

"With strawberries and whipped cream!" Chip added.

"Ooh, ooh," Carlos interjected. "Or you can make banana pancakes. They're even better!"

"Well, Chip," Arlie said, pulling out the box of baking mix from the cupboard. "Looks like it's fried banana cakes. We're fresh out of strawberries and whipped cream and… Yikes!"

"What's wrong, Daddy?" Chip asked.

"My watch just buzzed, and I almost dropped the pancake mix."

"I didn't hear it," Carlos said.

"Me, neither," Chip added.

"That's because it just vibrates on my wrist. Excuse me, guys. Someone's trying to call me, and my phone is in the bedroom. I'll be right back."

The door opened before he had a chance to touch the knob. "I think your first wife is trying to call you," Charlene said with a scowl, then chuckled. "You left your phone on the nightstand and I was awakened by zippity doo da, Abby's ringtone."

Arlie gave Charlene a quick kiss on the forehead. "Sorry. I forgot to take it with me. Go ahead and get back to bed. I'm going to make pancakes for the boys. I'll wake you when they're done, if you'd like."

"A good lover and a cook, too? You're so full of surprises, Arlie Biggar."

"Washing dishes and being a short order cook got me through college. That and a few other odd jobs I'd rather not discuss," Arlie said, adding a wink, "But let me call Abby and see why she's bugging me so early in the morning."

"If it's this early, then it must be important." Charlene took the box of baking mix he still held out of his hands. "I'll take over the breakfast chef duties, so you can give Abby and the Anchorage Police Department your full attention."s

"Thanks, dear. You're a keeper!" he said, patting her bottom as she turned to walk away.

"Couldn't get rid of me if you tried," she called back.

Arlie ducked into the den to make his call. "Hey, Abs. What's going on?"

"Um, I just got the DNA results from that real weird package that was forwarded to me while you were recovering from your coma."

5

"Yeah. So? Isn't that your job: analyzing weird and random items?" Arlie asked, then closed the door. "What kind of weird are we talking?"

"Scalps."

"What?" Arlie yelped, glad that he had shut the door and Charlene and the boys were now listening to classic country music on the radio while making breakfast.

"Well, you remember how we caught Gordo and found his stash of scalps?"

"Yes. I remember hearing about it after I came back around. That bloated monster cost me my spleen and robbed me of six weeks of my life. I'll never forget him! From what I recall of that conversation, Gordo's cousin — my skinny little lifesaver, Lucky — led the APD to the creep's lair. There was enough evidence to pin a whole slew of skelpings and murders on that big bag of cow manure. Gordo De Luca was, and still is, out of the picture so it couldn't be him, right?"

"Well, that's what I thought, or hoped. I called and he's still in solitary confinement. I guess he doesn't play nice with others. Actually, this box only had one scalp in it. It was in a big zip-lock bag with the words 'random transient' written on it with a black marker. No fingerprints, either."

6

"Okay. So why did you say there were 'scalps' in the package?" Arlie asked, his nose twitching at the sweet, bready smell of banana pancakes cooking.

"The two other bags in the same box looked empty, but they were labeled in the same handwriting, like they were just waiting for the scalps to be added. I found a single hair in each one of them."

"Well? Are you going to keep me guessing? Come on, Abby. I have a family now and they're making breakfast. Let me enjoy being a newlywed, will you?"

"Arlie, one said Marc Audie." She paused, then added, "The other said Daywalker."

"Oh, shit."

"Yeah, oh shit — your street name. The box came in the day after you were married. It usually takes a while to identify the DNA, but I already had your DNA profile in the computer from when I ran the paternity test on you and the boys. I asked for and received Marc's DNA from a cheek swab. After that, it was just a matter of matching the known data against the hairs. I told Marc what it was for and asked him if I should tell you."

"And what did he say?"

"He said if you were the one who had knowledge about a potential hit, and he was the intended victim, he'd want you to tell him. So, I'm telling you. Someone wants your scalp."

"Wants it again," Arlie said, and groaned audibly, his hand automatically reaching for the scarred-over wound on his left side. "Gordo already did his best. He just didn't count on scrawny little Lucky to take him out with a fire extinguisher. What else can you tell me? How did the box get to you? Was there a return address, a postmark, a tracking number? When…"

"Slow down and give me some credit for basic diagnostic skills. The box was mailed from the downtown Anchorage post office the day before I received it. It was mailed directly to me here, care of the Department of Public Safety, and the only return address was the initial 'G.'"

"But when?"

"I told you. Ten days ago. That means there's no way that Gordo could have mailed it. From what I heard, he's been locked up in solitary confinement for almost two months. I guess he has some real anger issues…"

"Yeah, tell me about it." Arlie ran his fingers through his hair, moving his morning love romp-tangled locks out of his face. "Let me do some thinking and I'll get back to you. Looks like I'll be returning to work sooner than later. Crap. I really did want a honeymoon, even if it was just here at the house while the boys were at school."

Knock, knock, knock.

"Pancakes are ready, Daddy," Chip called out.

"Yeah, and we got a new bottle of syrup for 'em, too," Carlos said. "It's apricot!"

"I'll be right there," Arlie said to the closed door, then turned back to the phone. "Give me a couple hours, at least."

"Take what time you need, Arlie. Only you, Marc, and I know about this right now. Cap's out of town for the rest of the week, or I'd fill him in, too."

"Later, lady. Be safe."

"You, too, little brother."

"Right," Arlie said, then laughed. "Thanks for leaving it on a bright note."

"What was that all about?" Charlene asked as she presented him with a plate stacked with three pancakes, all sporting smiles made from sliced bananas.

"Looks like I'm needed back at work," Arlie said, a slight grimace tangling his otherwise happy face. "I really wanted to stay home for a while longer, but as they say, duty calls."

"I love you, Arlie, and I've declared to everyone who's important to me that I want you in my life forever but having you around the house all day can be a little…" Charlene squirmed, wiggling her bottom so only he could see, "Maybe a little too much of a good thing. I was thinking that maybe I should start looking for a job, too."

"Wait. What? I thought you wanted to try being a stay at home mom for the first time in your life."

"Come on, boys. Finish up your breakfast, then go get ready for school. Remember to make sure you have your homework in your backpacks." She turned to Arlie and continued. "I've been a stay at home mom since we moved in here nearly two months ago. Or, should I say, since I moved in here with the boys. You've only been here a few days. Actually, I was glad I had the excuse to get out of the house and go see you at the hospital."

"Old folks home," Arlie corrected with a chuckle.

"Extended care facility," Charlene countered. "Whatever you want to call it, I realized that if I had to just sit in this house for seven hours while the boys were in school, I'd go nuts. I did some research and I think I'll either volunteer for the school district or go back and update my legal clerk certification. I don't want to be a lawyer, but I can still help others by filling out forms and knowing where and when to file the proper documents for all sorts of legal procedures."

"But if you worked for the schools, you'd have the same days off as the boys, right?"

"Our boys, but I could still be flexible with working for myself. Plus, I could do as much as I wanted from home. Coffee shops are great places to meet for signatures. No office required."

"As long as you're able to be here for the boys when they're out of school, or make arrangements for same, I'm good with whatever career direction you want to take. I'd love to say I'll have your back on taking care of them, but as a cop, my hours are erratic. Nothing is set when you're a detective." He reached over and patted her belly, balancing his plate with his other hand, "And whatever career will be best for you when the next baby comes along."

"Legal aide and consultant is starting to sound better all the time."

Chapter 2
Skate Date

When an ice skate blade presses against the ice, a thin film of water is created and melts the ice. This acts like a lubricant and allows the blade to glide. Figure skating blades usually are made of tempered carbon steel that are first heat treated. The blades are coated with a high-quality chrome. In recent years, lightweight aluminum and stainless steel blades have also become popular. Carbon steel blades are softer than stainless steel blades. https://www.thoughtco.com/questions-about-figure-skating-blades-1281766

Arlie took a deep breath as he looked at the wide concrete and tile building. Smaller than some facilities, but size didn't matter here, either. The Department of Public Safety had the latest equipment and some of the most skilled analysts, including Abby. Arlie wasn't back to work as a cop yet, but the tingles were starting. He was itching to get back to the team.

"Hey, there, Lisa!" he said to the lady at the desk, a very pregnant short-haired blonde who had attended the police academy with him and was evidently on light duty. "Looks like you're due to take maternity leave soon—very soon. Do I need a visitor tag, or do you remember who I am?"

"Pregnancy doesn't affect intelligence or memory, Arlie. It's after the kid is born and you're sleep deprived that the brain goes dotty. Go on in. Just sign here first. Abby told me you were probably going to grace our corridors before lunch. Looks like you were a little eager to get here. By the way, Cap mentioned he would really like it if you came back to work at least a week before I took off to have this little soccer player. I swear, he's already kicking field goals..." She bent forward and grabbed her lower belly. "There he goes again!"

"You'll be the third, maybe fourth person to know when I'm coming back—after my wife and Cap. I'm hoping I'll be released to return to work full duty on Friday. Too much time off is tiring!"

Lisa pushed the security lock release button and let him in to see Abby. "You'll remember what being really tired is like soon enough, I'm sure," she said to herself softly.

And there she was, as tomboyish as ever, her hair pulled back in a stark ponytail, the collar of her red plaid flannel shirt showing over the neckline of her white lab coat as she

13

leaned into the monster piece of electronic equipment, her face practically glued to the eyepiece of her electron microscope. "So, Abby, what do you have for me?" Arlie asked as he peered over her shoulder.

"I was trying to see if there was something special about the address label on the box. It's the generic kind you can pick up in the lobby of just about any post office in the country, though. It's cluttered with so many fingerprints that even if one was left by the sender, I'd need to know who it was first, and then see if it matches one of the thirty I've isolated so far. Nope, it looks like I've come to a dead end with this part of the puzzle. I might as well hang it up until something else comes in...hopefully less gruesome."

"Gruesome never bothered you before. What's going on?" Arlie asked, backing away as she turned toward him, away from the high dollar piece of equipment.

"It's always bothered me. I've learned to emotionally compartmentalize just about everything sordid that comes my way, though. I've told myself so many times that what I do here in the lab will get—and keep—the creeps off the street. All was fine, then this 'G' comes after you and Marc. I thought it was Gordo, but it can't be him. He's out of the picture, locked away for life. When this box came in, suddenly, it was like 'G' was coming after me. Sending a challenge directly to me, letting me know he was skilled—experienced, willing and ready to take more scalps—and that two of my best friends were the target." She involuntarily shuddered and didn't even try to hide it.

"And that's why you called me little brother?"

"Yeah, well that kinda sorta slipped out, but I'm glad it did. Speaking of brothers, though, there's a guy like you from my past who's coming in later today." Abby ran her fingers through her hair from the middle of her forehead back, incorporating that one strand of cowlick that always pulled out. "How do I look?"

"Gorgeous, like always. But tell me more about this other brother-type person. Do you think I'll like him? What does he do? Why is he coming to Alaska or has he always lived here? How come I've never met or heard about…"

"Slow down, detective," Abby said, playfully covering his mouth with her purple neoprene gloved-hand. "I used to work with Billy back in Greensboro before I came here."

"Does that mean he works with the police department there?"

"Yup! He's a detective, too. Pretty sharp, and cute, too."

"But does he have these gorgeous auburn locks?" Arlie asked, then chuckled as he flipped his hair back with a feminine flourish.

"No, but he does have a red-haired son. Come to think of it, I think Mac is about the same age as your boys, maybe younger."

"And…" Arlie asked, giving her the third degree with his single drawn-out word.

"Billy told me he needed a break. Well, actually he said he missed me and figured there'd still be snow in Alaska in late February, so it would be the perfect time to bring Mac out to discover snowshoeing and meet me. But I knew what he meant."

"Are you sure you're not reading enough into this? I mean, a guy coming out to introduce his son to you… Maybe he has more than brotherly feelings for you and he doesn't know about you and Mimi. You and Mimi are still okay, right?"

"Duh! Yeah." Abby giggled. "I'm not his type, anyhow. He has a partner and they've been together for at least five years that I know of. They were married as soon as it was legal in North Carolina. I think they're Rock of Gibraltar solid.

Or at least, I hope they are."

Buzz. Buzz.

"Abby, you have a couple of good-looking gentlemen here to see you. Is it all right if I let them in? I mean, you don't have anything visible that would unsettle a youngster, do you?"

"Nothing but an empty cardboard box, Lisa. Go ahead and show them in."

Arlie stood back while the raven-haired young man, handsome enough to have been a model, gave Abby a full-body hug that ended with a lift-and-spin flourish.

"How's my wee Abby doing?" he asked, then looked her up and down, appraising her new svelte figure. "And it looks like half of you is missing…"

"Only the ick half. You know, the 'I'm frustrated with life so I'll eat myself out of a freezer full of ice cream just to prove I'm a survivor' part?"

"Abby, you're more than a survivor," Arlie interjected, "You're a savior, too. And I'm living proof of your life-saving skills. That's what, twice you've saved my life in two months?" Arlie turned to Abby's shocked friend. "Hi, I'm Arlie Biggar. In case she didn't tell you, this clever little munchkin

17

developed a little device that, although it takes the privacy out of my life, alerts her when my heart rate is too high or low, or my brain waves go nutso. We don't tell just anyone about it, but she told me you were her first brother. I thought I'd tell you about it, so you could be proud of her, too." Arlie reached out and shook the hand of the man who looked to be about thirty.

"Billy Burke Melbourne. Glad to meet you. My professional name is Billy Burke, but I'm a Melbourne by blood." Billy took hold of his young son's hand and brought him in forward. "This bashful young lad is my son, Mac Melbourne."

The red-haired boy reached out to shake Arlie's hand. "I have a bunch of other names, too, but I like Mac best. It's easier to write, too. Daddy says I'm really smart, but Dad," the boy looked up at Billy, "says I'm not supposed to tell people."

"Yes, son. They'll figure it out…or they don't need to know. Just be a kind and helpful person. That's what's important. Now, you need to say hi to Abby, too."

"Hi, Abby, too. I thought your name was just Abby," Mac said, then hunched his shoulders up and started giggling. "I made a joke, huh?"

All four of them laughed together, then settled down when Billy saw the box on the table. "What's that? Did one of Santa's Christmas presents get lost and you're trying to figure out where it goes?"

"No," Abby said. "It was mailed to me—by first and last name and department—from the post office branch a few blocks away. It had some," she said, then whispered the word, "scalps," then spoke up again, "evidence in it. The return address just had an initial on it, no name."

"Don't tell me it was G," Billy said, his eyebrows crowded together in concern.

"Oh, shi…shoot!" Abby replied.

"Bang!" Mac said, then started giggling into his hand again. "That's what we say at home when someone says shoot."

"Mac, I need to talk to Abby and Arlie about some work stuff. You know when I bring you into the office sometimes, you sit in a chair and quietly draw pictures? Can you do that now?" Billy pulled a little paper notebook and pen out of his pocket. "Oops! Wrong one. That one's mine. Here's yours. Why don't you draw some animals and put their names underneath? We'll look them over later, when we're at lunch."

19

"Okay. I'll be right here when you're done!" Mac said, then got comfortable in the padded desk chair in the corner and started softly singing 'Old MacDonald' to himself.

"Abby, how long ago did this come in?" Billy asked, then picked up the box and turned it over.

"Almost two weeks ago. Arlie was still recovering from being stabbed by a guy named Gordo. Gordo had threatened to," Abby whispered the word, "scalp," then returned to her soft voice, "Arlie and take it as a trophy. I guess there was a contract out on him." Abby's big dark eyes grew even wider as realization hit. Her hands flew up to her mouth to cover her gasp. "Shoot!"

"Bang!" Mac said, then resumed his singing.

"Don't mind him," Billy said. "He's not really listening. At least, I don't think he is. It's a conditioned response to the word. I've even heard him say it in his sleep when his other dad and I are talking and happen to say the word."

"I thought Arlie was out of danger with Gordo in jail. I never, ever thought that maybe someone else wanted the bounty on him. Sorry. Poor word choice."

Arlie rubbed his stubble-whiskered chin. "No, it's actually a very accurate word." He reached up and ran his hand through his hair. "Just not a good topic. So, if G isn't Gordo…"

"Before you get too carried away, Arlie, I need to tell you that this G has been a problem for almost a year in the Greensboro area. For some reason, vagrants were targeted," Billy said.

"Did they all have long hair?" Abby asked.

"Not necessarily. They were homeless people who lived in the woods. Even from the first box with the, ahem, hairpieces in it, not one of them was identified as a known street person. And no bodies were ever found, either. Believe me when I tell you, the shelters downtown quickly filled up with Woodsies. They haven't been too keen on returning to their tents in the woods, either. The erstwhile campers have been huddled in doorways and under bridges, keeping close to streetlights and cops ever since the first reported incident. Actually, the charities and social programs are grateful that those in need were staying so close by. They're making progress with a lot of them, finding jobs or social programs to fit their needs. Come to think of it, though, I don't think there's been an incident in at least a month. I'll check in and see. Where's the signature?"

Abby pulled out a glass slide with the original shipping label sandwiched in between. "Look familiar?"

"Unfortunately, yes. I'm not a handwriting expert, and it wasn't my case, but your replacement in forensics passed around a photocopy of the original box label to all the guys and gals, just in case we came upon something like it when we were out and about. Nothing. Zip. Nada. We don't even know if we're looking for a man or a woman, much less what the monster looks like."

"Can I draw a monster, Papa?" Mac asked.

"Yeah, sure. Just make sure you draw him in a cage so he doesn't hurt anyone," Billy said. He pointed to his ear and grinned. "Sharp kid. Monsters is another key word for him."

"So, do you have your schedule of places to visit set?" Arlie asked with a feigned smile, eager to change the topic of discussion.

"We have a week to take in the sights. I wanted to make sure I got him to a zoo or museum where he can see real arctic animals, either live or preserved. He went ballistic when we came through the Anchorage Airport. Who knew that moose were so huge? They had a fantastic variety of stuffed bird and animal specimens around every corner.

Having those huge displays of stuffed birds and mammals might bother some folks, but it's the safest way for people to realize how unique and treasured these indigenous animals really are."

"I agree. Say, how would you and Mac like to meet up with me and my family this evening for ice skating, and then some Mexican food?" Arlie asked. "Maybe we can talk Abby into lacing up, too."

"No, no. Not me. Ice and I don't get along. Besides, I have plans, but you guys get together. Just be ready for some stares. Three little red-headed boys, all the same size, running around together..." Abby shook her head, then pulled out a file so she'd look busy.

"Your sons have red hair, too?" Billy asked.

"Yup. Just like mine. Where'd Mac get his?" Arlie asked, then cringed. *Dummy! You know he's gay and has a partner! The boy is probably adopted, and Billy might not even know what the parents looked like!*

Billy chuckled when he saw his new friend's unease. "Both Mac's biological parents had red hair. His mother died a few hours after he was born. His biological father is actually his godfather. Mac not only got red hair and blue eyes from him, he also got his height. Benji's six foot seven. I don't doubt Mac will be much shorter than that. He's already as tall as some kids two years older."

"Yeah, I got three dads! Billy, Peter, and Benji!" Mac crowed. "I don't have a mom, but I have an awesome grandma. I call her Nana, and she bakes me cookies and reads me stories..." Mac bent back to his notebook. "I'm going to draw a picture for her, too."

"So, did you happen to bring ice skates with you from North Carolina?" Arlie asked Billy, then chuckled at the bright boy, intent on his artwork.

"No, never thought about it. Doesn't the skating rink rent them out?"

"Where we're going, there aren't rental stations…" Arlie said in a deep, eerie tone, then laughed and brought the levity back. "I don't think they're too pricey to buy, and you won't be paying a fee to skate at the outdoor rink in downtown Eagle River. Just make sure you both bundle up in layers and wear hats and gloves. Oh, and you'll probably get a good deal on the skates at Sportsman's Paradise. End of season sales, and all that."

Billy turned to his son. "Hey, Mac. Do you want to go ice

skating this evening?"

Mac finished tearing the two pictures out of his notebook. "Is that like rollerblading?" he asked Arlie.

"Yeah. Pretty much. Except that you're on a blade, sort of like a knife, instead of wheels. Why? Do you know how to rollerblade?" Arlie asked, squatting down next to the charming and well-behaved child.

"Yes, sir. I can. And the bottom of an ice skate's like a knife? Why isn't it called ice knifing, then?"

"Well, I guess because back in the old days, they couldn't afford metal for the gliding surface. They used wooden blades to 'skate' across the ice. Ice skating," Arlie explained, grateful that he had read the Hans Brinker story when he was younger.

"Okay," Mac said, accepting Arlie's answer with a word and shoulder shrug. He handed a sketched drawing to Arlie, then got out of the chair and gave the other one to Abby. "I made one for you, too."

"Wow! You are quite the artist, young man. This looks just like the stuffed musk ox in the airport terminal. And you even spelled his name correctly. How old are you?" Arlie asked, truly amazed at his skill.

"I'll be five in June," he said. Young Mac didn't even wait for the comment but addressed it before Arlie said anything else. "Yeah, I'm real tall for my age."

"Oh, a teddy bear," Abby said as she fawned over her picture.

"Yeah, just like the one pinned to your jacket. But teddy bears are pretend animals. They look like koalas, but koalas aren't really bears," Mac said. "They're marsupials."

"Yes, yes, Mac," Billy said, and pulled his encyclopedic son close to him. "Now that we've said hi to Abby and met her friend Arlie, let's go shopping. We're going ice skating this evening and we both need skates. I wanted to go to the zoo today, too, but we might do that tomorrow instead. I promise you, we'll get there eventually."

"By the way," Arlie said, "you'll get more stuffed animals to look at when you're shopping at Sportsman's Paradise than at the airport. Maybe we can all do the zoo another day. At least at the store, he won't have to look behind trees and snow piles to see the critters. Lots of animals are hibernating now."

Chapter 3
Surprise!

The United States Federal Witness Protection Program, also known as the Witness Security Program or WITSEC, is a witness protection program administered by the United States Department of Justice and operated by the United States Marshals Service that is designed to protect threatened witnesses before, during, and after a trial. As of 2013, 8,500 witnesses and 9,900 family members have been protected by the U.S. Marshals Service since 1971. https://en.wikipedia.org/wiki/United_States_Federal_Witness_Protection_Program

"Hey, Arlie. Are you back to work already? I thought you were going to take off at least the rest of the month," Marc said.

"I came in to talk to Abby about our biggest fan, G. She didn't have anything new. Yet. I wonder how in the heck he got a hair from both of us? We don't even see the same barber!"

Marc grinned at Arlie and nodded. "Yeah, well, when was the last time you saw a barber? Nah, I don't even want to think about the G situation right now. I have my own problems. So, are you here doing research on your own time then?"

"I told Cap when I left last December that I'd consult for free until I was able to come back to work full time. It's sort of my 'I can come into the office and snoop around without filling in a time sheet' card. So far, nothing but more questions—like my first one, how did he get a hair from both of us?"

"Well, we did have lunch together a couple weeks ago. Char was with us, but if someone checked out the booths after we left with a—pardon the expression—fine-toothed comb, he could have come up with a few stray hairs. Since her hair's long and dark, yours is red and long, and mine is short and black, it would be easy to tell them apart."

"Yeah, well, he'd have had to have that booth sanitized before we came in. I don't think that's likely, but you might be onto something. By the way, Marc, have you had any trouble with old Papa De Luca or any of his boys lately? I'm beginning to think he might be this G."

"Nope, we haven't had any trouble from the old man, his crippled kid, or any of those snotty grandsons. Not even a harassing phone call about how we wrongfully put his two healthy sons in prison. Actually, one of my informants asked me if I'd heard anything regarding him. If you want, I can ask around and see how long he's been incommunicado."

"I'd appreciate it. By the way, I just met a friend of Abby's, a detective who used to work with her in Greensboro, North Carolina. Seems like G's been on their radar for about a year. Same profile and signature as this creep. He suddenly disappeared about a month ago. No more murders or skelpings. It's their gain and our loss, I'm afraid."

Arlie suddenly clutched his stomach, then stumbled over to one of the chairs in the lounge.

"Are you all right?" Marc asked, then grabbed a bottle of water from the employee fridge and handed it to him.

"Dang! Why didn't I think of it before?" Arlie took a long drink of the icy water, then sat forward, elbows on his knees, intent on his crime-fighting friend. "I don't think I ever had the chance to tell anyone, but I overheard Lucky reaching out to G on the phone the day I got skewered by Gordo. Lucky knows who G is!"

"Isn't he in witness protection, though? He's so far off the grid, he might as well be in Australia on walkabout."

"He and I left on good terms. I mean, the kid saved my life at the risk of losing his own. I'm pretty sure he'd clue me in if I could just connect with him. I don't even know if he's aware that G is on the rampage. Abby said the department has been able to keep everything about the death of the vagrant out of the paper, including his scalped head, but the guys in the shelters and on the street know all about it. However, no one knows about the scalp coming in to the department in a bag signed 'G.' When Cap gets back, I'll see if there's a way I can at least talk to Lucky."

Marc snorted. "Well, good luck with that one."

Chapter 4
How to make a redhead

(ScotlandsDNA believes that everyone who carries one of 3 variants of the red-hair gene is a direct descendant of the first redhead ever to have it – two variants originating in West Asia around 70,000 years ago, and a younger variant originating in Europe around 30,000 years ago. Most carriers of the red hair gene variants don't actually have red hair themselves and may not know they carry it, but ScotlandsDNA has developed a test to let parents see if they might have red-haired children. For a child to have red hair, both parents must be carriers of the recessive gene and there is a 25% chance that their offspring will have it. http://www.abroadintheyard.com/red-hair-genes-directly-inherited-from-first-redheads/

Later that morning:

The smell of yeast bread rising and just a hint of cinnamon greeted Arlie as he walked into the toasty warm kitchen from the chilly garage. He inhaled deeply. The only smell better than a bakery was that same comforting aroma coming from your own kitchen. His curvy wife was bent over the counter, kneading a cream-colored lump of dough into submission. "Hey, honey, I'm home! It sure smells great in here!"

Charlene reached up and pushed the hair off her face with the back of her flour-covered hand. "Hey, yourself," she said with disdain covered with irritation, then forcibly swallowed the automatic smile that arose every time he was near her. She stood back and readied herself emotionally, tamping down her tenderness and pulling on her cast iron panties to deliver the stern message that had been eating at her all week. "You know, Marc told me a lot about what to expect with being married to a cop, but you never brought it up. I don't mean to sound needy, but do you think you could try to spend a little more time with me and the boys?"

Charlene bent back to the breadboard and continued kneading the bread dough, this time slamming it down, intentionally using more force than when he had walked in.

"I'm sorry. I should have called earlier when I realized it was a possibility that I'd be working," Arlie said, then stood close behind her and gave her a peck on the cheek. "The good part is, right now I'm not on active duty. I'm still on medical leave, so I can come and go as I please as a consultant. When I do start working again, any extra hours I put in will be comp time since they don't want to pay overtime. That means if, or when, I work long days and weekends, I'll be able to take an extended break. Sort of like I'll be banking hours."

"Good Lord, I wished you worked banking hours," Charlene said, then started to laugh at his unintentional miscommunication.

"Banking hours, as in I'm working extra hours that I'll be able to use down the road. You know, like for a vacation."

"Or a stay-cation, with all the phones and computers turned off. I still have to finish studying before taking the test to get my license," she said, then turned the bread into a hastily oiled over-sized bowl. She tossed a damp tea towel over the top of it, then sighed. "That's it for an hour or so. Let's go talk. The boys won't be home for a little while, so it's just you and me."

"Honey, if all we have is an hour, I'd rather not spend it talking…"

"But, but…" she said, her protests cut short by the distraction of his tender kisses behind her ear.

"Just know that I'm never spending time at the bar or chasing skirts," he murmured.

"Unless you're working undercover…"

"But I don't have to be anywhere but here with you—just the two of us—at least until the boys come home."

Charlene pulled back. "What happens when the boys get home?"

"Oh, I meant to tell you," Arlie pulled away and took a deep, humbling breath. "I sort of invited a couple of Abby's out of town friends to dinner and ice skating." He noticed her pout and decided their afternoon delight would have to wait.

He took both of her flour-dusted hands in his and kissed her knuckles. "Honey, I probably should have called and asked you, but it was one of those spontaneous moments that I didn't want to pass up. Forgive me?"

"That depends. What sort of friends and where's dinner. Oh, and do I have to skate, too?" Charlene pulled one hand from his and rubbed her bottom. "I'm still sore from three days ago."

"Mexican food and one friend's another cop—a little older than me—and his four-year-old red-headed son. The boy's younger, but about the same size as Carlos and Chip. Cute kid. You'll love him."

Charlene wiped her hands on her apron, then wrapped

34

them around Arlie's neck. "All right. I always did have a soft spot for redheads. Come on," she said. She took his hand and placed it on her breast. "Let's go see if we can make a little ginger sister for the boys."

Chapter 5
New Friends

The first ice skates were developed about 5,000 years ago and were made from the leg bones of large animals such as horses, ox, or deer, and were attached to feet with leather straps. The first metal blade ice skate was found in Scandinavia and was dated to 100 A.D. A thin strip of copper was folded and attached to the sole of a leather shoe.

"You're right," Billy said as he walked up to Arlie and his family. "Eagle River is very small—less than a tenth the size of Greensboro— but easy to find. Everyone I've encountered seems to be just as friendly as any Southerner I've ever met. Hi," he said, extending his hand out to Charlene, "I'm Billy, a friend of Abby's from a few years ago." He paused, then amended his statement. "I'm still her friend, but we worked together up until a few years ago. She seems to really like it out here. Too bad. I could use her skills again."

"Oh, no, you don't," Arlie interjected. "You're not getting her back... Oh, hi, Mac. Come on out and meet my sons. This one's Chip and this is Carlos."

The bashful boy came out from behind his father's legs, glanced up, then all the boys mumbled, "Hi," to each other, then went back to clinging to a parent.

"Let me guess," Charlene said, "You're all hungry and just can't wait to get to the chips and salsa, right?"

"Yeah! Yeah!" the boys said, all three of them hopping up and down, their shyness wiped away with the promise of salty snacks.

"Let's skate first and work up a big appetite," Charlene said, then produced a fistful of granola bars. "But in case you're too hungry to put on your skates…"

"Thanks, Mom," Chip and Carlos said and took a snack bar each.

Mac looked up with a sheepish grin, "Thanks, Mom," he said softly as he took his, then hunched his shoulders up and giggled. "I've never called anyone Mom before."

The six-pack of friends and family weaved past two young couples leaving the rink and established themselves on the wooden bench. "Do any of you need help?" Charlene asked the boys.

"We got this," Arlie said. "How about you two?" he asked Billy.

"I'll help Mac if you want to get yours on," Charlene offered her fellow brunette.

Mac held out his skates to her. "Here, Mom," he said and giggled again.

Charlene accepted them with a smile. *He's so charming!*

"Thanks," Billy said and pulled the hat down over his chilly red ears, then bent forward to lace up his skates. "Dang! It's cold! Aren't you skating, Charlene?"

"I might work up the nerve to get back on the ice if I get too cold just sitting here and need a warm up. I fell pretty hard the other day. I'm a bit out of practice." She saw his look of confusion. "I spent the last seven years in Arizona. I missed a lot of rink time."

When she finished lacing and tying Mac's skates, she looked at the boy's hands. "Where are your gloves? You can't get on the ice without them."

Mac looked around frantically. "I had them in my pocket. I shoved them in real deep, but they must have fallen out." He looked back toward the parking lot and saw a little old lady, all bundled in fur and scarves, waving his gloves in the air. "There they are! I'll go get them. Don't worry. I'll be careful."

"But the guards are still on," Charlene called after him,

"So, don't try to skate yet."

Mac step-waddled toward the figure bundled in shades of gray fur and wool. "Thanks for finding my gloves," he said, then turned to walk away.

"Um!" the old lady growled, then shoved a brightly colored pin at him.

"A teddy bear?" Mac asked.

"Uh huh," she huffed, nodding to make sure he understood her graveling tone.

"Thanks, but no thanks," Mac said, then handed it back to her. "I'm not supposed to take anything from strangers."

He turned to leave, then felt a strong hand on his shoulder.

"Uh uh," she growled, shaking her head, increasing her grip. "Here," she grunted and tried to stab the pin into the front of his jacket.

Mac squatted down, dipped his shoulder low and twisted out of her clutch, then ran back to Charlene as fast as he could in the clumsy skates, trying not to cry.

She put her hands on his shoulders to steady him after his awkward beeline to her. "What's wrong, Mac? I thought that sweet little old lady found your gloves."

"She's not sweet! She's mean and ugly and she pinched me and got mad when I wouldn't take her present and, and…"

Mac rushed into Charlene's now opened arms and sobbed into her puffy coat. She looked up and saw the hunched-over woman climb into a road grime-gray sedan. The woman with the scarf-wrapped face backed away without checking mirrors or looking behind her, then pulled onto the main road without pausing, nearly causing a pile up as cars in both directions slammed on their brakes to avoid hitting her.

"She's gone now, sweetie. Why don't you go skate with the guys and I'll talk to the dads about it when we're at supper? Don't worry about her. I'll stay here and make sure she doesn't come back." Charlene reached into her pocket and brought out a bright pink palm-length cylinder. "I have pepper spray and I know how to use it. No one's going to mess with one of my boys," she said, then gave him a kiss on the top of his knit cap. "Go out there and see how much rollerblading and ice skating are alike. I've done both and…" She paused a moment. "Actually, the ground is just as hard whether you fall on ice or concrete. But there's so much ice around here in the winter, we might as well enjoy it!"

Billy skated up just as Mac had composed himself. "Is everything all right," he asked, then looked to Charlene for verification.

"He's fine. Some creepy old lady tried to give him a present and got ticked when he wouldn't take it from her. She's gone now. You guys go have fun. I'll stay here and watch out for two-legged varmints."

"That means we'll talk about it later, right?" Billy asked, then bit his bottom lip.

"That's exactly what it means."

"Yeah, and she has pepper spray and she knows how to use it, huh, Mom?"

Billy mouthed the word "Mom?" then replied, "Yes, son. Mom's a tough one. Come on. Let's go show these other boys a thing or two about skating."

***

"Hi, again," the waitress said when she saw Arlie. "Looks like a family reunion."

"Nah. Just a couple out of town friends," Arlie answered, then headed back to the corner booth, his usual spot.

"So, do you come here often?" Billy asked.

"About once a week, sometimes more if I set up a meeting

with a contact or two. It's discreet yet open."

"Right," Billy drawled. "Hide in plain sight."

Arlie pointed his finger at him and said, "Bingo. Now, everything on the menu is good, but I suggest we start with the huge sampler appetizer. I don't know about you men, but I worked up an appetite."

"I may not have been skating," Charlene said, "but I burned off a lot of calories keeping warm."

"And staying diligent," Billy whispered.

"Can I get you some appetizers and drinks to get started. And would the boys like to color?" the waitress asked.

"Yeah, yeah!" the boys chorused, gladly accepting the cups of crayons and coloring sheets she set down in front of them.

"Root beer?" Arlie asked as he looked around the table. "One, two, three… Okay. How about a pitcher of root beer, six mugs, and a super supreme appetizer? That'll get us started."

"So, Mac, Charlene told me that a woman at the rink was mean to you," Billy said. "Tell me what happened?"

Mac looked at Charlene, then all around the table, his eyes staying low, watching everyone's hands, then his head popped up to make sure no one was laughing at him.

"You're not in trouble, son. Remember how we talked about stranger danger? You did great, running back to an adult you know. Charlene told me what happened, but I want you to tell me in your own words."

"I think she took my gloves out of my pocket when I walked by her the first time. They were shoved in there real far because I didn't want to lose them. She saw me looking for them and waved them at me. When I went to get them, she grabbed me by the shoulder and tried to make me take a present. It was a teddy bear pin, just like the one Abby has. You know, the one I drew a picture of?"

Arlie and Billy nodded. "And?" Billy prompted.

"And when I said I couldn't take a present from strangers, she tried to stab me with it!" Mac looked down at his hands, idle next to his coloring sheet. "I think she was trying to pin it on my coat, but it poked me! She said, 'Hur,' but she meant 'here,' I think. She didn't talk too good. She was like a monster!" Mac's hands flew up to his face and his shoulders started to heave with sobs.

"There, there," Billy said as he held him close, comforting him. "She's gone now. I don't think we'll ever have to worry about seeing her again."

"Promise?" Mac asked, his nose sniffing back the tears.

"I promise to do everything I can to protect you from her. And Arlie and Mom will, too. I don't see any way she'll be back in our lives. Never say never, but she'll never bother you again if I have anything to do with it."

"Hey, boys," Arlie said. "How about I give you some money for the claw machine? Mac, Carlos is a pro on those games. Just tell him which toy you want, and he'll snag it for you." He put a fist full of quarters in Chip's hand. "Watch out for each other, all right?"

"Yes, sir," he said. "But I know you can see us from this table…"

Arlie leaned over and whispered in Chip's ear, "Yes, we know that, but Mac is younger than you and Carlos. Having a big brother-type to stand right next to him while he's at the game machine will make him feel better. He got scared this afternoon."

"All right," Chip whispered back. "I'll be the big brother today. Thanks, Dad."

As soon as the boys were distracted at the toy-filled cubicle, Billy asked, "What's going on? You were as white as snow when Mac mimicked the old lady's voice."

"That was no lady. That was G."

Chapter 6
At your service!

The Municipality of Anchorage is the largest city in Alaska (although not the capital). It spans 1961 square miles which includes JBER (joint military operations Base Elmendorf, Fort Richardson, and Kulis Air National Guard), Eagle River, Chugiak, Girdwood, Indian, and a few other small 'towns' which embrace their local identity, and most of Chugach State Park. At 61 degrees north, it is farther north than Oslo, Norway and Saint Petersburg, Russia. It lies within nine and a half hours of 90% of the industrialized world and is nearly equidistant from New York City, Frankfurt, and Tokyo.

"Here are your drinks, sirs and madam, and your appetizer is in the oven and will be out shortly." The bearded young man with short red hair, blue eyes, and thick glasses winked at Arlie as he set down the pitcher in front of him. "Is there anything else I can get for you?"

Arlie glanced up, started to say, 'No, we're fine,' then froze before the first word was formed.

"Oh, my God!" slipped out before Arlie could stop it. He turned and searched the dining area, the panicked look on his face causing both Billy and Charlene to scour the area for whatever was terrifying Arlie.

"What's wrong?" Billy and Charlene asked at the same time.

The waiter chuckled. "Well, I guess if anyone could see through me, it would be you, right, Daywalker?"

"Don't call me that," Arlie hissed, "for your own sake. Only guttersnipes and crooks call me that, and the last I remember, you were neither."

"Ach, I'm just messin' with you, Arlie. Looks like you have quite the family. Three sons? Last I heard, you only had two. Then again, you got those two in, what, less than a month? You sure work fast."

"Who's this?" Charlene asked Arlie.

"Yeah, what she said," Billy echoed.

"Tell them your name," Arlie said. "I'm curious to know what moniker they bestowed upon you."

"I told them I wanted my own first name since no one knew me by it anyhow. I'm Louis—or Louie—Lachlan. I'm going with the Scottish ancestry angle to match my red hair. Plus," he whispered, "the nickname for Lachlan is Lachy. Close enough to Lucky for me."

"You're an imbecile, Louie," Arlie said, then looked around, making sure others weren't interested in their conversation.

"This is the kid who saved my life just over two months ago," he whispered to Billy and Charlene. He turned back to the former Lucky De Luca and asked, "Why didn't you relocate to a different state, or at least a different town?"

"Eagle River is a different town from Anchorage—sorta," he replied. "Besides, Alaska kind of gets in your blood. That and everyone else who had it in for me for helping you is either in jail or laying so low, they're in a different latitude. A few of them scrambled back to Costa Rica, I think. Something about looking for a bunch of cash that Rosa stole from Alonzo and Papa."

Louie aka Lucky winked at his last remark, making both Arlie and Charlene's stomachs knot. *Did Lucky know they had Rosa's money, that she had bequeathed it to Charlene to watch over Carlos in the event of her death…which came two days after she had signed her informal will?*

Arlie decided it was best to change the subject. "Let me properly introduce you to my wife, Charlene Biggar, and our friend, Billy Burke."

Arlie's face split into a big grin as he remembered that

earlier today he had wished he could find Lucky, and now the young man was standing in front of him. *Thanks, Lord!*

"I've actually been looking for you, Louie. Or at least I was getting ready to start looking for you. Now's not a good time for either of us to talk, I'm sure. We're at a family dinner and you're a server. What time do you get off work? Can we meet up to catch up on old times?"

Lucky Louie's face fell at losing the upper hand. Did he do something wrong? Or get caught selling pirated movie downloads? "Um, I get off at 7:00. Why don't you pick me up across the street, at the skating rink?"

"That sounds like a plan, Louie Lachlan." Arlie reached his arms out and stretched, tapping Billy and Charlene on their shoulders with pats of appreciation. "Welcome to Alaska, young man," he said with a wink, "the land of fresh beginnings."

***

"Mom, Mom," Mac called out as he ran to the table, clutching four stuffed animals to his chest. "Look what Carlos got me." He turned to Billy. "Daddy, can Chip and Carlos be my brothers?"

Billy's mouth worked between a grin and a frown, finally

settling on a smile. "How about if we call them cousins?"

Mac scowled but didn't reply.

"You know, don't you, Mac, that if Peter and I adopt again, you might get a brother or a sister. Since neither he nor I have siblings around anymore, these boys might be your only chance at having cousins." *At least in this century! You already have first cousins in the 18th century!*

"Oh, okay. But can I still call Charlene Mom, even if she's not? I kinda like saying it…"

"I don't mind," Charlene said. "And I am Mom to Chip and Carlos, so already answer to it."

"All right! New family dynamics, as fluid as needed for those involved," Arlie said. "This calls for a toast." He grabbed the pitcher and topped off all the glasses of root beer. "Here's to family, whether by blood or by choice. May our lives be long and boring!"

"Here! Here!" Billy cheered, and clinked glasses all around. "A long boring life to a cop is pure heaven!"

Arlie settled back into the booth, then spoke softly to Billy. "Yeah, well my life might get interesting here in another couple of hours. I don't think Lucky Louie knows that G is in town. He sounded like he believed everyone had left Alaska."

"Thanks for dinner and asking us to come skate with you, Mom. I hope we can see you again before we go back to North Carolina," Mac said.

"That would be nice," Charlene replied, then bent to give him a hug good-bye.

"Arlie, thank you, too," Mac said. "Oh, and I drew this picture for you. I know you're a detective like my daddy. This is what that mean old woman's face looks like. She's real ugly, but just saying ugly doesn't describe her very good."

Mac handed Arlie the coloring page with his original art work on the back, then put his hands on his face. He pushed his nose to one side and pulled his lower lip in the opposite direction. "It looked like someone put her face on wrong," he mumbled through his skewed mouth. He sighed and let his face relax back to normal, then finished his description. "She was mostly covered with a dark scarf, so I couldn't see her hair. I'm sorry, but I forgot to look what color her eyes were, but they were sure scary!"

Arlie held up the picture. "Wow, Mac! You've got quite the gift for drawing. Hey, how about you go with Charlene and the boys to the car for a few minutes. She's planning a trip to the zoo for all of us and you might have some ideas on a few other fun things to do, right, dear?"

Charlene winked at him, letting him know that she knew he needed a minute or two to speak to Billy alone. "Come on, boys," she said. "Let's all crowd into the back seat until the dads are done talking. We have a zoo day to plan!"

"Wow, you sure got a good one," Billy said as he watched Charlene lead the three boys away. "How long have you two been married?"

"A couple weeks," Arlie answered. When he saw Billy's shock, he gave him an ultra-brief background of their relationship. "I only met her a couple months ago, and yes, I'm the father of both boys, but only Chip is her son biologically. It's complicated, an interesting story for another time. Right now, I want to bounce the few things I know about G off you."

"Sounds good to me," Billy said, "But let's go further into the corner where we can see who's coming in without being seen. I doubt that freak of nature will be returning, but..."

"Yeah, I know. Second nature. Never turn your back to the door," Arlie said. "Now, something that Mac said really got my attention. Well, it all did, but this part had relevance."

"You mean the teddy bear pin thing?" Bill asked.

Arlie snorted as he laughed, trying to keep it in. "Wow! You're sharp! Yes, the teddy bear pin. Abby has one. One of us needs to contact her and find out where she got it. I'd say somehow or other, G gave it to her so she could spy on what she's doing in the lab."

"Gee, and here I thought I was getting a vacation from detective work. No, don't worry about Abby and the pin. You have enough on your plate right now. I don't want to call her about it, though. She lives in Anchorage and we're staying at a bed and breakfast not too far from her. I'll pop in on her tomorrow morning and discreetly dispose of, or at least temporarily disable, the pin so it's not transmitting."

"I've developed a few of my own little devices, so I know how they're constructed. I bet the eyes on that little bugger are cameras. A mic or two could be hidden anywhere and the transmitter could be integrated into the body." Arlie paused. "No one gave you or Mac anything since you've been here, have they?"

"I bought the skates, hats, gloves and food from the usual retail places. Nothing out of the ordinary. As you saw, Mac's pretty sharp about not accepting anything from strangers.

How about you and your family?"

"I'll verify when I get home. Lord, I hope G doesn't know where we live."

"You got my number. Put me in the loop on this one. I'll call back to my guys and gals in Greensboro and get them up to speed on this." Billy looked around anxiously. "On second thought, I'll pick up a disposable phone and call in. I'm suddenly leery of everything."

"Give me your phone," Arlie said, holding his hand out.

Billy gave it to him, then scooted back in the booth to see what his new cohort was going to do with it. Arlie took his smartphone out of his inner pocket, did a few taps and swirls to open an app, and scanned Billy's phone with it, using his phone like it was a TSA wand at the airport. "It's clean," he said, then pointed it all around their booth. "This part of the restaurant's clean, too."

"Is this an app you bought or created?" Billy asked. "And can I get one?"

"Some guys collect coins or build models. I collect algorithms and create apps. They're not for purchase, but before you leave, I'll set you up with a few. Right now, I should probably get back to Charlene and the boys. I want to make sure they're all safe and sound at home before I come back here to meet up with Louie."

"I'd better get going, too. We're pushing ten o'clock Greensboro time. I'm sure Mac's ready for pajamas, a relaxing story and bed." Billy brushed his hand through his hair in frustration. "Come to think of it, that sounds good to me, too."

***

Marc unlocked the door to his hangar and looked around. Nothing looked amiss. He got back in his truck, reached up and pushed the button on the remote for the overhead door, then drove inside. Not saying a word, he pulled open the bottom drawer of his tool box and took out a fat padded manila envelope. He couldn't help but grin as he pulled out the dark gray fabric bundle. He took his phone out of his pocket and slipped it in the Faraday pouch, folding the top closed to make sure all incoming and outgoing digital information was blocked. Dottie knew where he was. If there was an emergency, she would call Remo and he'd run over and get him. Not many guys lived in their hangars, but Remo was both an aircraft mechanic and watchman for the small out-of-town airport. He was also the unofficial neighborhood snoop, checking to make sure doors were locked and windows intact as he walked his dog twice, sometimes, three times a day. Surveillance cameras were good, but the sight of a burly man walking his mammoth Rottweiler were the deterrent needed at this remote, end of the road airport.

"Ah, nice and deserted. Nothing sweeter than an empty hangar when you're looking for peace and quiet."

The off-duty deputy marshal cranked the classic country radio music high enough to drown out his worries but kept it low enough to hear his own thoughts.

He hadn't thought about it when he was with Arlie earlier but—outside of their luncheon at the Mexican restaurant— there was only one other time when the two of them were together in the last three months. They had both gone out to the shooting range last week to check out Marc's custom reloads. He had picked up Arlie at his house in the truck. This truck. If someone had picked the lock and got in the cab since that time, there were bound to be plenty of his hairs— and maybe a few of Arlie's—on the seat. Arlie was the only long-haired redhead who had ever been in his truck. All the culprit would have had to do was give the seat a quick once over with a shop vac or lay down a strip of tacky tape, and he'd have the hairs he needed for those plastic baggies of intimidation sent to Abby.

Now it was time for some old-fashioned Sherlock Holmes-style sleuth work. Marc took the magnifying glass with the built-in light out of the top drawer of his oversize toolbox and scanned the keyhole on the driver's side door handle. He always used the key fob with the electronic remote or the touchpad to unlock the doors, so any signs of forced entry or marks on the lock from being picked would probably be from G. Not a scratch on the keyhole, new or old. Rats. That would have been too easy. He didn't have his field kit with him, but he did have foot powder. A few sprinkles of it on the numbers should show something. Marc poured some powder in his hand and blew it onto the keypad.

Voila!

Prints all over the place. He only needed to use two of the five numbered pads when he unlocked the door, and all five of these had been touched. He grabbed the packing-tape dispenser from the shelf and pulled off a length of clear tape. Ever so gently, he pressed it on top of all the powdered fingerprints, then pulled it off just as diligently.

"Looks like Abby has a little research to do." Marc looked

over at his phone, still in the pouch. He didn't trust it not to be tampered with. He would catch up with Arlie later and have him scan it with his app. Even though he always had his phone with him—and it had never been out of his sight, accessible for tampering—he'd err of the side of caution and speak to Abby in person. Or he'd call her after Arlie had given him the all clear for his phone. This was literally his scalp on the line, He wasn't taking any chances.

***

"Are you sure you'll be all right? Do you want to call Marc?" Charlene asked, fixing him with her 'I'm the mom in charge and no nonsense allowed' stare. "I'm sure he'd be happy to provide back up. You do remember the last time you went in on your own, right?"

Arlie rolled his eyes at her tacit reprimand, then paused. *Last time you did this, you almost got killed!* "You're right," he said. "I'll give him a call."

Arlie called Marc's house phone then his cell phone. No answer on either. He wouldn't leave a message. Marc would call back as soon as he saw a missed call from him. It was what they did for each other rather than waste time retrieving voice mails.

One last shot: a text. 'R U there?'

Nothing.

"Well, dear, either Marc is asleep or so deep undercover that he can't reply. This is just Louie, though. The kid saved my life, testified against his family, and joined witness protection to get away from them. I'm sure I'll be fine. Besides, if Marc is simply away from his phone for a bit, he'll call me right back." He gave her a peck on the cheek. "Thanks for being so sweet to Mac. He sure was taken with you."

"Pbbt! No problem there. I always did have a soft spot for redheads. He may have two dads and no mom, but he doesn't have a problem with being around women. I guess he's very close to his grandmother and is missing her quite a bit. Now, about this other thing…"

"I promise I'll be careful. You have Marc's number, and you and Dottie are close. Why don't you give her a call and see what her hubby's up to? If I call, she'll know I want him to come work with me and she'll make an excuse for him."

"Coward," Charlene said, then shook her head. "All right, but you owe me one."

"Yeah, well, I'll have a nice big one for you when I get

back. Promise. I'm going to get there a little early, though, and do some scouting around. Make sure all the doors and windows are locked and call me after you talk to Dottie."

"I will, but just to be on the safe side, would you wear your vest?"

Arlie patted his chest, then reached in the hall closet and took out his Kevlar protection. "I guess my brain was saying this wasn't a potentially dangerous situation, so I didn't even think about it. Yes, dear, if it will ease your mind, I'll suit up." He pulled off his flannel shirt and put the vest on over his white cotton tee shirt. "Now, no fair reading any of your romantic suspense novels while I'm gone. Pick up one of those with puppies and flowers on the cover. You're less stressed when you read those."

"Call me when you're done, before you leave the restaurant, so I'll know all went well."

"I will."

"Promise?"

"Okay. I promise I'll call before I leave the meeting."

"All right." Charlene gave him a slow, passionate kiss good-bye, her inner insecurity fearing this could be her last one.

"It's gonna be all right," Arlie said again, softly this time, "but if your fear gets me this kind of kissing, that's okay, too."

Charlene smacked his shoulder with the end of her fingertips, missing the full slap because he had anticipated it and pulled away.

He leaned in and took a quick kiss. "I'll be back before you're half-way through the third chapter," he said, then slipped out the door, waiting for the sound of her dead-bolting the latch before he got in his car.

***

A few people still lingered at the skating rink, mostly teenagers hanging out: girls giggling on one side, boys hooting and slapping each other on the other. A typical gathering formation of high schoolers, too bashful to pair off and talk, but eager to share the same air space with each other. Arlie squinted into the dim spots of the otherwise bright park, looking for anyone lurking behind bushes or cars.

Nope. Just loud hormonal teenagers.

Arlie went back to his car, started it up, then moved it under the brightest streetlamp in the area. He cranked the heater up to its highest setting, then backed it down a notch when it got too hot for his chilled fingers. He pulled off his damp gloves and swiped and tapped his phone to check for a missed call or text from Marc.

Nothing.

Thunk! Thunk!

Arlie looked up and saw Louie smacking his windshield.

"Can I come in? It's colder than a witch's tit out here."

What a dolt! Can't he think of something wittier to say? Hmph. At least he knows to come in out of the cold.

Arlie hit the switch, unlocking the doors.

"Damn! I knew I should have worn boots today," Louie said, and slipped off his sneakers to warm his toes directly in the stream of hot air blasting out from the under the dashboard heater duct.

Arlie looked down as the stench of stinky feet permeated the car. "You didn't even wear socks?"

"Nope. I missed doing laundry last week, and no matter how bad it gets, I won't wear the same pair of socks more than three days in a row." Louie reached down at his right and found what he was looking for, pushed it, and reclined the seat almost all the way back. He put his hands behind his head and grinned as he settled into full relaxation mode. "So, Arlie, what can I do for you?"

"Tell me all you know about G," he said, watching Louie's face for fear or surprise.

He got both.

"G...Gee?" Louie sputtered, almost choking in shock. He reached down and pushed the seat position button and sat back up. "Why do you want to know about G?"

"Are you going to tell me or not?" Arlie asked. He wasn't going to threaten or cajole him. At least not yet. First, he wanted to see how far the kid's loyalty went. Was he going to be honest or lead him into a dark closet full of bat guano?

"Nobody, but nobody outside the family knows about G," Louie said, his eyes shifting back and forth as if he was sure he was being set up and a wrong answer could mean death.

"And that's why I asked you. Until just recently, you were family. So, tell me." Arlie slipped into bad cop mode, letting his eyes narrow as in 'I know more than you think I do, so you'd better tell me everything...or else!'

Louie took a deep breath, then blew it all out. "Do you have anything to drink?"

Arlie reached into the backpack Charlene had forgotten to bring in the house and brought out a small box of apple juice. "Will this do?" he asked.

The anxious young man took it from him hesitantly, squeezed it to make sure it wasn't frozen, then pulled the straw off the side of the box and jabbed it in the top. "Not exactly what I was thinking of, but it'll help." Louie took his time in sipping the juice, then tipped it every which way, trying to get that last dribble, slurping Scotch whistles until he was satisfied he had emptied it.

"That's all there is, Louie. Time's up. Tell me."

"G's Papa's first wife—Alonzo's mother—so I guess that makes her my almost grandmother. At least, she would be if Alonzo was really my father."

"Keep going," Arlie said, then opened his window a crack to let in fresh air. Louie's stinky feet were giving him a headache. He turned his back to the side window and gave his informant his full attention. "You already told me Alonzo wasn't your real father and that Alonzo had your mother killed."

"Well, he kinda did and he kinda didn't. You see, Papa is the boss of everything. Sort of. G is the one who tells him what to do. I'm pretty sure he's scared of her."

"Tell me more," Arlie said, and arched his back, uncomfortable with both this new revelation and his awkward position.

"I only met her once, briefly. She's the mother of all Papa's sons, but she bailed on him just after Slinky was born. You know about Slinky, don't you? The kid whose legs didn't work?"

Arlie nodded. He really didn't know much more than Papa had a crippled son who was born after Alonzo and Luca. He didn't care about him, though. He wanted to know about G.

"So, after Slinky was born, G split sheets and left Papa to take care of three young boys by himself. Supposedly, she went to help her old man on his marijuana grow site in North Carolina. Story goes she went down and took over the business, cut out her father completely. No one's heard from the old guy since. Papa figured she probably knocked him off and buried him in the south forty. It didn't make him no never mind—said he never cared for the greedy old bastard anyhow."

"So..." Arlie prompted, his head tipped to the side, letting his two-legged database know he didn't want any more stalling or ancient information.

"What?" Louie asked, squirming in his seat. "That's who she is."

"And after she took over the grow operation…"

"I guess she did okay for a few years. At least, word was that Papa was glad she wasn't trying to micro-manage him all the time like she had when they were living on the same estate. I guess she kept busy with growing and selling weed and her, ahem, hobby until she got popped and sent to the slammer."

"What was she arrested for?" Arlie asked, then reached over and kicked the heater back up a notch.

Louie laughed, then shook his head. "Her hobby! Seems like she'd make arrangements for underaged runaways—street kids, whatever—to come work for her. She'd have her way with them until she got bored. Then she'd call in for some Midwest muscle to do a little housecleaning. She'd take a break from playing around with boy toys, then send her chauffeur out again, looking for another pool boy to deflower."

Louie looked up at Arlie's red hair. "She was particularly fond of gingers," he said, and winked.

"Ew!" Arlie grunted, disgusted at both the implication and the perversion.

Louie, encouraged by Arlie's aversion to the topic,

continued his story with enthusiasm. "Yeah, well they finally busted her. I guess one red-headed kid escaped, testified against her, and they sent her up the river for," Louie counted fingers on both hands, then finally gave up. "She got busted in '97 or '98 for life. The cops dug up eight bodies in her south acreage. She may not have been the one to shoot them, but she did put out the contract for someone else to bag and bury the boys."

Rather than hold it in, Arlie rolled his shoulders in discomfort, intentionally feeding Louie's ego.

"Of course, once she was in prison, she returned to being the bossy bitch, calling in to Papa at least once a day, making connections and demands, telling him how to do everything and what to do to whom. You know, generally making the old guy miserable. She still had her Midwest connection, so he didn't dare cross her. She didn't make any friends in the slammer, either. I don't know if you know it or not, but women in the big house are even meaner than men, or so I've heard. G mouthed off one too many times and got cut up pretty good. The broads rearranged her face the first time. The second time, the butch queen herself went straight for her throat. Just about killed G, too.

"This go 'round, the prison doctor decided he'd better send her to a hospital rather than try and fix her up himself. He'd patched up her sliced and diced nose and mouth the first time, but he didn't want her to die from her injuries. I guess a few of the female prisoners had died while under his care and if one more died, he'd lose his cushy job. Imagine, having all the pussy you could want..."

Louie's carrot-orange beard split into a wide grin as he fantasized about having his way with incarcerated females. He reached down and rearranged his private parts as Arlie cleared his throat, reminding him to get on with the story. "Oh, yeah. G. They took her to the hospital, sewed her up, but the day before she was to be released, she disappeared. Poof! Gone."

"Where was this?" Arlie asked.

"Oh, they took her to Greensboro. It had the closest big hospital. Shoot! You should have seen Papa when he heard she'd bolted. I didn't know if he was happy or pissed. He had his contacts and could have gotten rid of her himself—and I wouldn't put it past him to have put the hit on her with that throat slasher on the inside—but I don't think he had to. G's pretty good at alienating folks for free. Two days after she disappeared, she called in to Papa. She couldn't talk, but she wrote out the words and had someone else read them for her. She let him know she was in charge again and wanted her cut and to be brought up to speed on all his dealings. Or else."

"Or else?"

"Yeah. That's what I said when he told me to watch out for her. He told me to play nice. Anything I wanted, I should go through her first. He'd tell me one thing, then shake his head, like he thought she was listening in on our conversations. I may not be the smartest fish in the pond, but I understood his cues."

"You're smarter than most folks give you credit for, Louie," Arlie admitted, hoping to sway him over to his side even further.

"Well, Papa may be the big fish…"

"But there's always a bigger fish," Arlie said, "and it looks like G is it, right?"

"Bingo!"

Chapter 7
Faraday

A Faraday cage or Faraday shield provides an interference-free zone for electronic devices, blocking electromagnetic material by utilizing a continuous covering (or mesh) of conductive material—such as copper—around an area. This physical 'aura' redirects electrical charges, keeping them from entering the cage's interior. The structure is used to protect sensitive electronic equipment from external radio frequency interference. Airports and laboratories have used these 'clean rooms' to test sensitive equipment for years. A Faraday bag is based on the same principle. The bag or satchel is made of flexible metallic fabric. It is typically used to prevent remote wiping of electronic devices seized in criminal investigations. Scientist Michael Faraday implemented his theory of deflecting these waves by devising a copper wire enclosure in 1836.

"Mac, I know we're both tired and ready for our book reading and quiet time, but remember how I told you that sometimes I have to put my personal life back here," Billy reached behind the car seat, "and do a job I really don't want to do right away in order to keep someone safe?"

Mac nodded, then stifled a yawn. "I remember. I guess that means that even though we're on vacation, you have to do something so someone doesn't get hurt, huh?"

"That's right, son. But tonight, since your nana and other dad aren't here, you're going to have to come to work with me."

Mac sat up straight, his fatigue overcome by the adrenaline of helping his father, the detective. "What do you want me to do?" His excitement suddenly dropped. "I don't have to shoot anyone, do I?"

"No! No, guns or knives or kicking or anything like that. It's just that I suspect someone is spying on Abby. Remember the teddy bear pin Abby was wearing?"

"Uh huh..."

"Well, Arlie and I think it's a spy camera!"

"Really?"

"Yes, and so we can't tell Abby what we think it is, or whoever is listening and watching on the other end will know we found out about it, right?"

"Uh huh..."

"So, we're going to do some acting. Anything I ask you to do, I want you to agree to. That means, say yes or yes sir.

And no arguing, all right?"

"Yes, sir. All right."

"That's my boy."

Buzz. Buzz.

Billy picked up his phone, still set on vibrate. The picture he had taken of Charlene and the boys popped up. "Hey, Charlene. How's it going?"

"How'd you... No, never mind. You're a cop and have your skills."

"Actually, when you were saying good-bye to the boys, I took your picture. I posted it to the phone number you gave me earlier. So, what's up?"

"I'm worried about Arlie. He left here a few minutes ago to talk to Louie, or Lucky, or whatever he's calling himself today. Anyway, he left without backup. He trusts the kid, and I do, too—sorta—but I got this icky, itchy crawly feeling going on. I can't reach his US Marshal buddy, Marc. I called Marc's wife and she said he was out at the airport. He likes to tinker with his plane's instruments. Real delicate stuff, so he turns off phones, radios, everything that might cause interference. That means..."

"That he can't get any phone calls or texts. So, do you

want me to go to the airport and find this Marc?"

"I don't know. You've got your son with you or I'd ask you to make a detour before going back to Anchorage and be Arlie's backup in Eagle River, or at least watch out for him. His meeting with Louie is supposed to be at the ice rink where we were earlier. Marc's at the Birchwood Airport. It's less than ten minutes away from me, but…"

Beep!

"Hold on, Billy, I think that's Marc on the other line."

Charlene put Billy on hold then came back to him. "It's Dottie, Marc's wife. He's fine. She said she'd send him on over to hang out in the parking lot at the ice rink to make sure no one sneaked up on Arlie or Louie. Thanks for listening to me whine."

"It's not whining when you're concerned for your spouse. Everyone needs that special friend. Thanks for letting it be me. I'll give you a call in the morning after we've had breakfast. We don't want to get to the zoo too early."

"Okay. Thanks again."

"All right, Mac, are you ready? I have to make a phone call or two, and then you have your first undercover assistant detective acting job."

"All right! Yes, sir, I'm ready. Did I say that right?"

"Yes, you did. Sit tight and I'll let you know what's next."

Mac grabbed the armrest and wiggled down into the seat. This was the best vacation ever!

"Hey, Abby! Are you still at work? Let's go have a bite to eat at the airport. Laticia made some of her apple strudel and made me promise to bring you over to sample it. And she said if we want coffee, we need to bring our own because she gave it up a few weeks ago. Oh, okay. I'm glad you decided to work late tonight. I'm about three minutes away. Lock up and grab your coat. We have a date!"

Abby was waiting at the main entrance for Billy and Mac when they pulled up. Billy got out and gave her a coy tap on the bottom. "You're so cute, darlin'. It's hard to keep my hands off you."

Before Abby could say a word, she saw his wink. The blatant sexual flirt was the signal they had agreed upon years ago to let the other one know they were being watched and/or listened to. Now was not the time to tell him what she had learned.

"Are you ready, Mac?" Billy asked as looked in the back seat. "We're going to a place near the airport to get some yummy strudel. Do you think you can handle a fancy dessert after that big Mexican dinner you just ate?"

Mac remembered he was supposed to agree to everything Dad suggested. "Yes, sir! I'm ready for more food!" he crowed a little too loud and with more enthusiasm than necessary.

"That's my boy," Billy said. "Come on, Abby. Let me help you with your coat."

Billy looked down and saw Abby was still wearing the teddy bear pin. He adjusted the opening of her coat over it, coyly blinding and muffling the suspected spybot.

After putting on her seat belt, Abby readjusted her jacket collar, exposing the teddy bear again. She looked over at Billy and sighed, hoping to read his expression. Were they out of hearing range yet?

Her subtlety went over his head, so she reached over and patted his thigh as he pulled away from the curb. Unaccustomed to a woman's touch, Billy's leg kicked out and he accidentally stomped the accelerator. He quickly covered his reaction with an excuse. "Your hands are like ice, darlin'. I guess I need to buy you some thicker gloves."

Mac snickered into his mittens, stifling his full-blown belly laugh at his dad's antics down to a low giggle.

"Is it warm enough for you back there, buddy?" Billy asked, then looked back and scowled.

"Yes, sir. I'm fine. I almost sneezed, but I caught it first."

"All right. Now, off we go to sample the best darned apple strudel in Alaska!"

"Do you mind if I turn on the radio," Abby asked, then looked over at Billy, hoping to see if she could read his response in the intermittent light of the oncoming traffic as they traveled the Glenn Highway to the airport.

"Whatever you want, darlin'" he replied, then reached up and gently touched her cheek with his gloved hand. "You're so cute," he repeated.

Well, that answers that! We're being spied on. It's not just eavesdropping, but someone—somehow—is watching us!

***

"You're back quick. How'd you enjoy your quiet time at the hangar?" Dottie asked, then leaned in and gave him a quick kiss hello.

"We're still newlyweds, aren't we?" he asked, glancing at the calendar on the refrigerator.

"Um, I guess so…"

"Then how about a proper—or maybe very improper—greeting?" Marc put one arm around her waist, the other behind her head, and gave her a probing kiss he normally reserved for the bedroom.

"Wah…" Dottie tried to say, but was stifled as he resumed his passion, pulling her closer, continuing his hungry lust-filled kisses until she was backed up against the kitchen counter.

Dottie looked up at him. "What got into you? Not that I'm complaining…"

"Just showing you how much I appreciate you," he murmured into her hair. He began nipping at her neck, little kisses with tiny bites that always set her afire. "The girls are still at the movies, right?"

"Um, hmm," she moaned. "Do you want to help me do the dishes?"

Marc shoved his sweatpants down, then spun her around and pulled hers down, too. "I thought you'd never ask…"

***

Moments later, Dottie pulled her sweatpants back up, then sashayed to the couch in the family room. She couldn't contain the huge grin of satiation to the hunger she hadn't even known she'd had, so didn't even try. "I'll never think about that sink the same way again," she said with a chuckle. "But if you don't mind, dinner will be a bit late. I need to recuperate. Yes, we're still newlyweds, but I doubt our passion will ever dim. When you're right for each other, you know it."

Marc splashed cold water on his face at the sink, then came over and sat next to her on the couch, pulling her head to his shoulder. "I did what I needed to do at the airport, then decided I'd better come home and check on you. I think someone might have messed with my phone, so I put it in a time out. I'm sorry. I hope you weren't trying to call me."

"Well, that was a hell of an apology, but no, I didn't try to call. But I did see a missed call from Arlie on the house phone, so he probably tried to call your cell, too. Charlene called me on my cell a little bit ago. She was worried because Arlie was going to your restaurant to meet some kid named Louie. I guess he's some guy from his past who he trusts, but Charlene's got that 'itchy, crawly, something bad's gonna happen' vibe going on, so she wanted you to go assist him as backup."

"So, is he already at the restaurant or do you know?"

"He probably is by now."

"Well, call Charlene for me, would you, and let her know I'm on my way. I'll hang out in the parking lot and make sure nothing fishy's going on. I'd call her from my phone, but it's out of commission for right now." Marc held up the copper-threaded phone pouch. "At least until Arlie can give it a clean bill of health."

***

All men are so dumb! You can lead them wherever you want with either money, sex, or food...or simply the promise of them.

G sat in the employee parking lot at the north end of the airport, comfortable in her plush but dirty and dented stolen Chrysler 300, waiting and watching to see where the two and a half geeks were headed. It had been easy enough to follow the techie nerd and the vacationing cop with that little wisenheimer kid of his, her headlights off, just in case. There was no way the cop could know he was being tailed. He barely glanced in his rearview mirror as he drove, his hands all over that forensic female. What did he see in that pathetically plain creature? She must be great in the sack. No. Wait. Didn't he say something about his kid having two more dads? What? Was he some sort of pervert?

Hmm. Three guys at the same time. Now that takes me back!

Whether this North Carolina cop also liked guys or not, it was obvious that pawing the ponytailed nerd wasn't upsetting his son in the backseat. The runt must be used to his horny old man. She couldn't see the ginger imp, but he only spoke up once, eager to eat more food. *Lead them where you want with money, food, or sex. This kid's too young to know about money or sex, but he'd probably do anything for a fritter.*

G shook her head, trying to incorporate all she had heard in the last week and a half into her plan. Never assume, especially when she had gleaned so much information. All she needed was a time and place to set up Marc and Arlie so she could take her trophies. Her backpack full of tasers would be enough to knock them down, even if her aim was off half the time. Once they were down, it was time for a slit and slice party. There would be plenty of time to bag, tag and brag about her trophies later. She'd be back in the intimidation game in no time. That marshal's short, spiky black hairpiece would look odd —almost like a beard instead of a scalp — but the Anchorage detective's flowing auburn locks…

Hmm. She hadn't seen hair that red since…

Crap! Benji! That punk who messed up my life twenty years ago was always hungry, lusting after food. This kid has the same insatiable appetite, same red hair, and is also from North Carolina. When he first met Arlie, Billy mentioned that the name of one of his kid's fathers was Benji. Double crap! No, wait! Hallelujah! I got me a legacy!

G's mood quickly dropped from elation to rage. She slammed her hand onto the dash, her guttural growl of pain and frustration stifled by the vehicle's road noise-resistant construction.

If Benji hadn't escaped with the help of that traitorous chauffeur, I'd have never been busted. And if I hadn't been busted, I'd never have wound up in that hellhole of a penitentiary.

G pulled down the visor and looked in the mirror. The bright white light was harsh, but even a soft rosy glow would have reflected a freak of nature. Nothing but a million-dollar plastic surgeon could repair what had been done to her three years ago. The red diagonal scars from the sharpened spoon shiv had faded to pink, but her nose and mouth no longer lined up. As long as she could eat and breathe, the prison warden wouldn't let her have reconstructive surgery. Then last month, that big black bitch botched her assassination attempt. G's paid 'friends' made sure she never got another chance to try again, either. *Rest in pieces, Bimbo!*

Would being dead have been better than being left without a voice. *Nah! Losing the power of clear speech was a small price to pay for my chance at escape. Maybe another million bucks or two can buy me a Mariah Carey voice. First, the reign of terror, then the ransom notes, then the big bucks! Papa's stash is peanuts compared to what is possible now!*

Chapter 8
It's cold outside!

The average high temperature in Eagle River in March is 30 degrees F, the low is 6 degrees. Snow is likely to be on the ground in the area from late October until mid-April.

"Looks like we have company," Louie said, nodding to the dark-haired, broad-shouldered man in Carhartts who was walking toward them with a confident stride, a wide smile on his face. "Is he a friend of yours?"

Marc tapped on the driver's side window. "Are you okay there, Arlie?"

"Yeah, we're fine," Arlie said, and stepped out of the car to have a private conversation. "I was just finding out about G from someone who has some inside information."

Louie thought about whether to wait in the warm, heated car or join the men outside, then decided he didn't want to look like a wimp, so stepped out into the breezy frigid air, immediately regretting his vain decision.

"Marc, this is Louie. Louie, this is Marc Audie, my friend and sometimes partner in joint venture projects with the U.S.

Marshals Department."

"Wow! You're a big dude. You didn't look so big when I was sitting in the car. I'll bet you know karate," Louie said, mesmerized by the deputy's dark eyebrows, wrestler-build, and tough man good looks.

"Yeah, I know Karate and his brothers Kung Fu and Jiu Jitsu, but their big brother, Common Sense, is my best friend." Marc reached out, squinted at Louie in his 'I don't want any nonsense from you, buddy' glare, and firmly shook the stunned young man's hand.

"And anything you can tell me, Louie, you can tell Marc," Arlie added.

"Uh huh. Okay…"

Arlie ignored Louie's sudden infatuation and brought Marc up to speed with the new information about G's background and gender.

"A woman? And she was married to Papa De Luca? Don't you think we ought to let Abby know?" Marc asked.

"Duh! Yeah, but there's no way to call her, even on a secure line, if she's wearing that cotton pickin' teddy bear broach. We'll have to go see her in person."

"Um, can I come, too?" Louie asked, his hand half-raised,

as if he was in a classroom and needed permission to interrupt.

Marc rolled his eyes at Arlie. It wasn't his decision, but they both knew the kid would be in the way.

"Sorry, not this time, Louie. We're just going to the crime lab, nothing heavy duty or exciting. Plus, I'd rather you stay away from Anchorage as much as possible. Being in the Witness Protection Program, I'm surprised they even let you stay in the state, much less the same municipality. Go somewhere and have something to eat besides tacos and margaritas for dinner. And buy some new socks!"

"Come on, Arlie. Let's take my truck and hit the road." Marc turned to Louie. "Nice meeting you, kid. See you around. Maybe."

Louie raised his hand and gave a weak wave. "Nice meeting you, too, Marc."

Arlie reached in, shut off his car's engine and locked it up, then turned to Louie. "See ya!"

"Yeah, sure," Louie sighed. *Such a wonderful specimen of male. Marc Audie…*

***

"So, Marc, what's really going on?" Arlie asked once they

were in the privacy of Marc's truck.

"I think my phone might be compromised. I know for a fact that someone broke into this truck, or at least tried. Pretty sure they got in, though. That has to be how he, rather she, got the hairs for those baggies of intimidation."

Arlie chuckled at his description, then said, "Give me your phone. I'll check out the cab, too. At least, as much as I can from here."

Marc handed him the Faraday pouch with the phone in it, then bit his lip. *Let's hope G couldn't get into it! There's too much sensitive data on it. My informants are as good as dead if they're found out.*

"Nope, your truck and phone are clean." Arlie held his phone up to Marc and ran it up and down his right arm. "Looks like you are, too." He looked at the Faraday pouch again. "Cool tool! As soon as we get to Abby, I'm snagging that pin and putting it in here. Let's see how G likes being bound in copper!"

***

The house was spotless, the cupboards reorganized twice, applications for online classes submitted… Charlene took her right knuckle out of her mouth. It had taken her years to give up nail biting, but she was getting close to starting again. That wouldn't help her situation, plus her hands would look ugly. She was too tense to even think about what she should do next, even after her early morning stress relief session with Arlie. Whether she went forward with her plan or not, she couldn't take her sons with her. She pressed and held seven on her smartphone. *I'm committed now!*

"Hi, Dottie. Hey, I'd like to ask a favor. Would you watch the boys while I do something special for Arlie?"

"Sure. No problem. I'll swing by right away. I just picked up the girls from the movies. We were talking about going out for pizza. What kind do your boys like?"

"Cheese, cheese, and more cheese for my little micelets."

"Same with the girls. I'll be there before you can stifle a sneeze."

Honk, honk!

Charlene looked out the kitchen window and saw Dottie's minivan pulling into the driveway. "Wow! That was fast." She pushed the end call button, then pulled on her coat, slipped on her boots, and walked out to talk to her new best friend and confidant.

Dottie rolled down her window. "We were already headed this way to ask you to join us for pizza. I didn't want to go home right away, so we decided we'd eat in at the restaurant. As you know, the more the merrier." Dottie took both her exuberance and voice down a notch. "Marc told me that when he and Arlie were done talking with his little buddy, they were going downtown to see Abby at the lab."

"Do you want to come in for a minute, or…"

"Nah, we'll wait in the car while you get the boys."

Charlene rushed inside and called out towards the family room, "Get your winter gear on, guys. You have a date. You're going out for pizza with Dottie and the girls."

"Pizza! Pizza!" they hollered as they stormed in and quickly began pulling on hats, gloves and boots in a fury of feet, fists and fingers.

"Here, let me pull up the zippers since you already have your gloves on." Charlene made sure they were completely bundled up, then herded them to the car. "Buckle up, boys."

Back to Dottie's rolled down window, Charlene pulled a twenty-dollar bill out of her pocket.

"No, I got this. I'm sure I'll need the favor returned one of these days." Dottie caught Charlene's eye. "Are you all right?

You don't look like you."

Charlene chuckled nervously. "Then who do I look like? Nah, I'm fine. I just wanted to do something for Arlie and I couldn't have the boys with me." *Don't let her even suspect you're going to spy on him!*

"Well, if you ever need to spill the beans before springing a surprise on your new husband, I'm here as a sounding board. I've been a deputy marshal's wife for only a year now, but there are a few things I learned the hard way—like you gotta let the guy do his job without bugging him about how his day went or asking all the normal wifey stuff. These guys have a different world to work in and we're not part of it. You shouldn't want to be in it, either. Remember, whatever it is you want to surprise him with, he's the trained professional. You're the loving wife. Don't think your concern for him is any substitute for the camaraderie and experience he has with others in his very specialized field, all right?"

"Yes, big sister," Charlene said, and swallowed an ounce of guilt at what she had already decided to do, regardless of her friend's warning. "Thanks for watching the boys. You and Marc plan a special day or night, then let me know date and time, and we'll have the girls over. I know they get a kick out of hanging out in the old playhouse, taking turns with the boys on the tire swing."

"Whatever you do, be careful. You're special to a lot of people, whether you know it or not." Dottie turned back to look at the boys. "Are you all buckled in and ready for pizza?"

"Yeah, yeah!" Chip and Carlos replied, their enthusiasm echoed by Dottie's daughters.

"All righty, then. Get ready for real Italian pizza baked by a genuine Greek!"

***

Before heading all the way into Anchorage, Charlene pulled into the skating rink to make sure the guys weren't still there. *You're being paranoid, Char! So, he forgot to call. He's safe plus he's wearing his vest. Even that app Abby let you download says he's fine. Good strong heartbeat, normal brainwaves. His tracker is still working, and he is, too. Stop being a freaky hormonal female.*

And there it was. Arlie's little Ford Focus was parked, fresh snow on the windshield, but Marc's big Toyota Tacoma was gone. The two of them had carpooled. What they had left behind, though, was Louie.

The scrawny redhead wearing a lightweight Seattle

Seahawk's jacket was jumping in place, stomping his tennis shoes to stay warm, ungloved hand out, trying to thumb a ride.

"Are you okay, Louie? You look a little cold. Can I drop you off somewhere?" Charlene asked. *Go ahead. Distract yourself with a good neighbor deed.*

"Hey, Mrs. Biggar!" Louie called out, glad to see a friendly face and a warm car. He rushed around to the passenger side and tried to open it. Charlene flipped the switch and unlocked the door.

"Auto locks. Don't take it personally," she said. "So, where are you headed?"

"I'm going into Anchorage. Your husband and Marc were just here. They're headed to Abby's lab, whoever she is." Louie stopped rubbing his hands together long enough to rub his chin in thought. "I hope they weren't talking about some lady's dog. Do you know an Abby and where her lab would be?"

'Um, yes, I do. Why didn't you just go with them, though? The truck's big enough."

"Arlie said he wouldn't take me because she might recognize me, but I just remembered something he needs to know."

"Who's she?"

"She's G, the woman who was supposed to be my grandma. I only saw her once, when Papa De Luca took me for a visit to see her in prison in North Carolina. It was about five years ago, and I had black hair and brown contacts back then. She's a very, very bad person," Louie said dramatically, hoping she'd be worried enough about her endangered husband to give him a ride all the way to Anchorage to deliver the new information.

"Okay, I'll take you there, but first, can I trust you?" Charlene asked, fixing him with her mommy glare of 'don't try and hide anything from me, buddy.'

Why does everyone look at me like I'm trying to pull one over on him or her? Louie nodded emphatically, then bent sideways to buckle up. "Of course, you can trust me. Your husband is breathing today because of me. He's cool—I like him. Oh, and by the way, I kinda found out that Judge Taylor is your old man. He's the reason I stayed out of major trouble and would never do much more than be a messenger for Papa and the others."

Charlene put the car in drive and headed for the highway.

"What do you mean?" she finally asked, not wanting to admit he was right about her father but wanting to know more of his story. After all, they had at least another 20 minutes of drive time and she wanted to fill her head with anything, even babble, rather than give in to her overwhelming fears. She looked at her phone again. *Cool, his vitals are fine, and he's still on his way to Abby's lab. Thanks for watching the boys, Dottie.*

"First time I got in trouble I was only twelve. The Judge was helping out with the at-risk youth group I was in and pulled me aside. He gave me a heart-to-heart talk like I'd never heard before. He told me to watch out for people who just wanted to use me to do their dirty work. He said I wasn't made to be a slave or a mop or," Louie snickered into the cuff of his jacket, "or the toilet paper to wipe someone else's ass with. Saying that really got my attention. He was a judge and all, but he was a real straight talker. That's what I like about Arlie. He never treated me like toilet paper. He even warned me about watching out for users, but I thought it was too late. Now with this witness protection stuff, I'm getting a fresh start. Oh, and just so you'll know. I don't treat anyone else like TP, either."

"I'm glad to hear it."

"So, why are you following him? Do you have some special information, too?"

Charlene remained mum, hoping he'd think she hadn't heard him. *How could she explain her paranoia? And should she?*

Louie spoke louder, prefacing his question with an exaggerated throat clearing. "Ahem. Do you have special information for him, too?"

"No, but…" Charlene didn't finish, but shook her head, trying to rationalize her hastiness to herself.

"Did he forget his gun, or even more important, to wear his vest?"

"No, but…"

She felt the weight of his hand on the jacket of her sleeve. "Missus B, Arlie knows what he's doing. By the looks of his friend, Marc, no one would want to mess with him, either. You need to let them do their job. There aren't enough 'No, buts' in the world worth endangering yourself. You wouldn't want to leave your three boys without a mother and a father, would you?"

"It's only two boys. Mac is just a friend." She took a deep

breath and took a quick sideways glance at him. "You might be right, but it's hard to explain, this gut feeling that something, or someone, is going to sneak up on him."

"Arlie's been a cop for how long?" Louie started counting on his fingers in a silly manner, losing track at four then restarted the enumerating again, adding a wink to get her to lighten up.

It worked. She relaxed her shoulders and shook her head in emotional defeat. *He's right and you know it.* "It's been quite a few years. In that time, he's outsmarted quite a few rogues and rascals, but..."

Louie put up his left hand, closing his fingers into a loose fist. "No buts. We can go to wherever that smartphone of yours says he is and be there when he gets out. I'm not going there to interfere, however—and that is not a but—he doesn't know about her cane of destruction. Plus, it might help him to know she's blind in her left eye. Sneaking up on her left side might make all the difference in the world."

***

"Laticia said to meet her over here," Billy said, his arm extended to show Abby the way.

Abby coyly slapped her keycard on the lock. She knew

they were actually in the maintenance part of the Anchorage airport, but she'd follow his lead and play along like they were meeting some woman named Laticia.

"I've never had apple studel," Mac said, rubbing his eyes to stay awake. "I bet I like it, though."

"I'll bet you do, too, buddy. It's just down this hallway and around the corner."

"Is the apple studel in here?" Mac asked as he stepped inside the shiny copper elevator car-sized room, his hands stuffed in his coat pocket, one hand polishing his agate shooting marble, the other playing with the mini troll doll Carlos had won for him at the claw machine. Keeping his fingers busy was how he made sure he didn't reach out and touch something he wasn't supposed to.

Billy let out a huge sigh of relief once he and Abby were inside, giving her a shy grin of apology for being so familiar. He shut the door, completing the copper wire blocking circuit. "That's strudel, son, and no, there never was any apple strudel. That's part of the acting we were doing so we could get to where we are now."

"Oh, thank God you were acting, Billy," Abby said, and planted her forehead on his shoulder. "I was pretty sure you were using our old signal that something was rotten, that we were being watched." She reached up and wiped her cheek where Billy had stroked it with the back of her wrist, then swiped it on the back of her coat. "No offense, but I feel like I need to take a shower."

"Did you get daddy cooties?" Mac asked, then giggled into his hand. "Girls at Sunday School have cooties, but I didn't know daddies could have them, too."

Billy looked over at Abby and shrugged one shoulder. *That's a good explanation, and certainly enough for a four-year-old.*

"Yes, I got daddy cooties. But don't worry; you can't get them from your own daddy, just someone else's." She rolled her eyes at Billy, then asked, "And I assume that because we're in this old dinosaur of a Faraday Room, we can now speak freely. So, what's going on, little brother?"

"Little? I'm older and taller than you, but regardless," Billy reached up and carefully unpinned the teddy bear broach from Abby's pullover sweater. "Tell me where you got this and how long have you been wearing it?"

"Huh? Oh, I got it about a week or two ago. Some deaf-mute woman at the mall was selling flowers. I bent over to see if her roses were fragrant, and she practically assaulted me. She put up one finger, asking me to wait, then wrote out a note. Hey, I may still have it in my pocket. Do you think it has her prints on it?"

"After being in one of your pockets? Nope. You've probably put the pin on and taken it off so many times that they're not on it, either."

Abby pulled a huge wad of papers out of her coat pocket and thumbed through the old receipts and tissues, then found it and read it out loud. "For you—to give you good luck. Remember to wear it always."

"And you did? Sorry, that was rhetorical, I think. Did you ever take it off?"

"Well, I didn't sleep or shower in it, if that's what you mean. And well, the day after I got the pin, I got a letter in the mail saying I won a trip for two to Costa Rica. I was going to let Mimi make the reservations, but unless I get more than two days in a row off, she'll have to go alone."

"So, you thought it was the good luck coming true from the pin and you decided to keep wearing it, right?"

"Well, yeah. You know I'm a bit superstitious…"

"Says the most dedicated and innovative forensics analyst

I've ever seen. Your skills and techniques got you far, but it's your insight that's closed a lot of 'impossible to solve' cases."

"Yeah. So fastidious and logical, and then I get duped into accepting a trinket that I wore every day to work…" Abby paled as her words faded.

"Yes, and that's why I figured we were in big trouble and had to get you away from your lab. G knows everything you've done, all the conversations you and Arlie and I've had, and how far we've come on the case."

"And Marc." Abby leaned against the cage wall, frustrated that she hadn't found out something earlier. "Crap, I hope he's all right. She figured out a way to get a hair sample from him, too."

"She's clever at cyber-sleuthing, all right…or at least has access to some high-tech toys. I don't know, but it looks like we may be one step ahead of the Greensboro crew on this now. I think they were looking for a male. It's late, but I should call… Nope. I can't call in here. Shoot…"

"Bang," Mac said without thinking. "Oops. Sorry."

"That's okay, buddy." Billy looked to Abby and huffed in frustration. "Let's get back to your lab. Once we get to a safe place, I'll make the call and let Greensboro know what we've found out."

Abby snorted, holding back a full laugh. "Well, tell me first; what did you find out?"

"That G is an older woman, not a man."

"Ha! I came to that same conclusion myself," she said, and smugly wiggled her shoulders in pride.

"What? How? And did you tell your suspicions to anyone while wearing the pin?"

"Actually, no. I spilled some Sulphur Dioxide on me late this afternoon and went home to take a shower to get rid of the stink. I took off all my clothes in the laundry room, then ran upstairs, buck naked..."

"TMI, Abby," Billy groaned.

"What's that?" Mac asked.

"I just want her to hurry up with the story," Billy replied. "So, you took a shower..."

"Yes, and while I was in there, washing my hair, I got the heebie jeebies and realized that it was just as likely that a woman did the scal... Ahem," she glanced at Mac and swallowed the rest of the word scalping, remembering how sharp he was in picking up on a conversation.

"It was just as likely that it was a woman taking the

scandalous trophies. Since I always have my phone in the bathroom with me for tunes, I called the Greensboro guys right away. I asked them if they ever pulled any full fingerprints from their, ahem, goods. Nope, but they ran their partials against the worldwide database. Nothing. Nada. Zip."

Abby pulled her shoulders back and did her pride wiggle again. "I asked them if they had run them against the short list of all the females who had recently escaped from custody. I think I made the poor guy feel bad. He was my replacement and already had big shoes to fill. He plugged in the data, and bingo!"

"And, and..."

"Geneva Shultz De Luca, the woman who got busted by a young kid named Benji MacKay. Ever hear of him?"

"That's my godfather!" Mac hollered, glad to be able to participate in the adults' conversation.

"And one of my best friends," Billy added. "I hope she hasn't tracked him down."

"As soon as we leave this room with her tattle-tale teddy bear pin, she'll be able to track us."

Mac took the break in conversation to ask, "What's this?" He held up a small copper box. "It looks like it was made out of pennies. Is it an inside-out piggy bank?"

"No, son, but I think it may have just 'saved' us a lot of trouble. I don't think anyone will mind if we borrow it. We'll put the pin in it for safe keeping, all right?"

"Can I see it first?"

Billy looked at Abby to see if she had any objections. She shrugged a shoulder minimally. "All right, but just watch out for the sharp end on the pin."

"Gee, thanks!" Mac moved into the corner where a bright light shone on the mechanical gauges, hoping to see something his detective dad might have missed.

Abby took the boy's distraction as an opportunity to engage Billy. "I don't think there's poison or any other chemicals involved with it or I would have noticed a reaction." She flipped open the top of the ornate copper sheet metal box with the word 'Faraday' stamped in it. "Looks like someone forgot to take this home with her."

Billy grinned at her use of the feminine designation, as if all folks who worked in the electronics field were female. "Or he bought one of those less expensive and more discreet copper wallets. That's what we use when we confiscate an electronic device in a bust. Still, this is pretty cool…

Thump! Thump! Thump!

"What's that thumping noise?" Abby asked, just as Billy looked toward the chamber door.

"Gotcha!"

Chapter 9
C-4

C-4 is manufactured by combining several ingredients with binder dissolved in a solvent. Once the ingredients have been mixed, the solvent is extracted through drying and filtering. The final material is a solid with a dirty white to light brown color, a putty-like texture similar to modeling clay, and a distinct smell of motor oil. It can be molded into any desired shape. C-4 is stable and an explosion can only be initiated by a shock wave from a detonator.
https://en.wikipedia.org/wiki/C-4_(explosive)

Hmph!

G tapped her tablet on the side of her hand, then shook it up and down and sideways. Still no GPS signal. *Where'd they go?*

Crap! Maybe the signal would be better outside of the car.

The perpetually angry woman opened her car door, wiggled and scooted out from behind the steering wheel until she was able to grab her right pants leg, and pulled herself free. She tucked the tablet under her chin, grabbed the armrest on the door, and stood up almost straight.

Damned cold weather! As if achy joints aren't bad enough in the heat, I'm practically crippled in this frozen hell hole! Just one more big score, and I'll be set. Papa didn't have as much money as I thought. Or he hid it well. Still, I'll soon have enough money to get a couple of vertebrae fused, a new hip, and a new face. She swallowed past the lump in her throat. *And a new voice. Plenty left over for a villa on the beach with the buffest physical therapists money can buy.*

G looked at her tablet again. Still no signal. She grunted unintelligible curses, not caring if anyone heard her. Now she'd have to go inside and find them. She fished around her inside coat pocket until she found it—the master keycard she had snagged from the janitor who stopped to help her jumpstart her car last week. *They won't find his body until the snow thaws. Unless the ravens finish him off first—then they'll never be able to identify the toothless troll!*

She grabbed the tablet again and swiped and tapped the history until she found the last known location of the spybot. That teddy bear pin was so tacky it was almost cute. It hadn't taken much to con it from that idiot developer. All it took was a few steamy online chat sessions with a phony profile and provocative photos, then a hired actress to pick up the little gift from her techno-gifted admirer, and she was set.

Who cares if that the bimbo ran off with him the next day? She was smart enough to bring me the spybot and programed tablet first. Neither one of them ever saw my face or knew my name. Money talking was the only sound little Miss 'Let's Party' cared about. And all Techno Dave wanted was perky boobs to play with.

She opened the back door, grabbed her backpack, and stuffed the inner pockets of her silver fox fur coat with as many tasers as she could. *Five should be more than enough. Two for each adult plus one for the runt.*

As soon as she slammed the door shut, she remembered it. She punched in her key code. *I can't forget my equalizer!*

G reached across the front seat to the passenger side and grabbed the top part of the cane. She had designed the odd-looking piece in the women's machine shop at the prison. That sucker of a warden thought he was being so gracious and generous, letting one of the inmates fabricate the wide-stance cane that would help poor little Geneva keep her balance. What he didn't know was that the outwardly simple design housed weapons and gadgets that would make James Bond jealous. *Damned male chauvinistic spy, anyhow. Taking advantage of women just because he's handsome and has a smooth voice. Probably has a little dick and that's why he never has the same woman twice — they won't come back to him!*

Even though the lights in the parking lot were bright and security cameras were sure to be recording her approach to the front door, G never looked up. Her lost little old lady ploy was only effective if she acted like she knew where she was going and what she was doing. She only claimed confusion if she was caught. *'I'm just bringing my grandson some cookies'* never fails to fool those sappy security personnel.

G patted her outside coat pocket, making sure the small bag of chocolate chip cookies was still there. Only once had she been asked to show the cookies, the time she had mistakenly given out the name of an actual person who worked in the facility she was robbing. Fast talking got her out of that one. *'Oh, my, my. I must have left the cookies in the oven. I'd better go home and take them out before I burn down the house.'* Dumb men!

The determined thief and murderess followed her tablet app to the last known location of the spybot device, grunting curses when walls and locked doors interrupted the straight-line path to her prey. *Why do they need so many layers of security, anyhow?*

And then there they were, directly ahead. The odd couple—Handsome Harry and Plain Jane—and that pipsqueak ginger brat. *Crap! I forgot the filet knife! I'll have to use my cane blade to gather my trophies!*

What in the hell were the three of them standing in? An itty-bitty copper cubical? It looked like an oversized disco lantern that should be hanging over a giant dance floor, dribbling out sparkly bright spots, but the lights were out. Or the idiots hadn't been able to find the switch to turn them on.

Thump! Thump! Thump!

Startled at the loud noise coming from in front of her, G jumped back, twisting her bum knee while trying to squat down and hide behind the drinking fountain.

She panted silently and composed herself. She was safe for now. Well-hidden. But it looked like someone else was joining the North Carolina rejects. She sniffed, then stifled a sneeze at their stench. *Not just a cop, but two cops!*

***

"Gotcha!"

Arlie laughed as he opened the latch and walked in. "Hey, there, Billy, Abby, Mac! Did we scare you?"

"Arlie?!" Billy looked down at the front of his pants. "Nope. Not much, anyhow. If you had, I'd have peed my pants. I wasn't expecting you. Come in and shut the door behind you, both of you. I assume this is a friend."

Marc squeezed past Arlie, latched the door behind him, then stuck his hand out to Billy. "Smart move, coming here to the old Faraday room. We didn't see anything suspicious on the way in, but at least we can be sure our conversation is private now. By the way, I'm Marc Audie, Deputy U.S. Marshal. Arlie and I work together at times."

"Billy Burke Melbourne, Greensboro Police Department, senior detective, but Billy or Billy Burke will get my attention." Billy stood on tiptoe and looked around Marc's shoulders, then added, "I hope no one here has claustrophobia. Free speech comes at the price of giving up ground space."

"Shoot!" Arlie said as he tried to raise his hand to slap himself on the forehead. He wiggled his shoulder back down and looked at the other adults. "I forgot to bring the Faraday wallet. Now how are we going to get that teddy bear spy pin out of here without her tracking it? I guess Abby can wear it out, but she'll have to be careful about what she says and what anyone says to her."

"We got you covered," Billy said, holding up the copper container. "I'm not sure what they wanted to store in this, but it's more than big enough to hold the pin."

"May I?" Marc asked and reached for it.

Billy handed it to him. "Not as discreet as a wallet, but it'll do the trick."

Clang! Clang! Clang! Clang!

Clink! Clink! Clink! Clink!

"Oh, shit!" Arlie said.

"Yeah, oh, shit!" Marc agreed as he followed the noise.

G was on the outside of the Faraday room, the huddled over old woman swiping her cane across the copper bars to get their attention, a wide lopsided smile splitting her wrinkled asymmetrical face.

Canned cops, how wonderful!

Young Mac quickly put the pin he had been inspecting in his pocket, then looked down. Maybe if he didn't see her, she wouldn't see him. He gulped, trying not to vomit. This was scary. Scarier than airplane turbulence or the monster movie he had watched at his friend's house last week. All he wanted was to be home, in his own bed, both dads taking turns reading his favorite bedtime story to him. He felt his father's hand, gentle on his shoulder, telling him without words not to worry. He'd take care of him.

No one said a word, the good guys plus Abby glancing at each other, letting one another know that they'd let G dig her own grave. Or a new prison cell. Hopefully, no shots would be fired.

Idiots! They're doing it on purpose, just to hear me try and talk. Don't make me mad, cops and kid. You won't like me when I'm mad…

Geneva held her thumb and index finger up, indicating the two-inch size of the teddy bear pin, then opened up her hand, gesturing that she wanted it.

"Oh, you want your little good luck charm?" Arlie asked snidely. "Maybe it will bring you better luck than you've had in the last—what?—twenty years."

"Here you go," Marc said, handing her the empty Faraday box.

G canted her head toward her shoulder, looking at the man who had said he was a deputy US Marshal. He was hot, but probably wouldn't be interested in her, no matter how much money she had. Or how beautiful she was. She glared at him. *Damned Federale!*

G snatched the box out of his hand, irate at just the reminder that she was no longer rich and gorgeous and able to command men's loyalties and peckers to do her bidding. She shook the box.

Empty!

"No, no, no!" Billy shouted as G raised her cane to Abby's face, ready to give her a new eye socket. "I gave the pin to my son to look at. Marc didn't know it wasn't in there. Son, show her the pin, and then put it in the box for her, all right?"

Mac put his hand in his pocket and pulled it out, flashing the teddy bear pin at the scowling crone. "Here, I'll put it in here for you," the scared young boy said, then took the copper box from Marc. He held the box close to his chest just as he dropped the pin to the floor.

"Oops!" He picked it up, waved it at her again, then opened the box and set it in, pushing the thin metal latch closed, bending the thin copper hasp to jam it tight. "It's safe in here," he said, then tentatively handed it to her, making sure he was far enough away from her that she had to hobble toward him, lowering her cane away from Abby's face in order to get it.

G shook her head at the bunch. *Too many people to tase. As soon as she got one idiot, another one would rush her. Besides, if this copper room is what stopped the pin from transmitting, who's to say it wouldn't stop a taser from working?*

She didn't have a gun and the two shots she had in her modified cane weren't enough to do anything but anger the cops. She reached into her pocket and pulled out the baggie filled with gray modeling clay. After she packed it into and around the door latch, she stuck in a piece of twine, then stepped back. *Let that smart aleck sack of misused estrogen figure out how to get out of there without blowing everyone to hell! It'll be half an hour, at least, before she or one of the others realize it's not C-4.*

Poof!

The smoke bomb G tossed exploded in front of the huddled mass of innocence and law enforcement. Their coughing and gagging covered the sound of her cackling as she disappeared down the hall.

"Hold on, everyone," Arlie whispered hoarsely. "Try not to cough."

Then he heard it for sure: the clack, clack, clack of her cane on the hard tile floors fading down the hall, verifying that she wasn't on the other side of the Faraday room. He reached out for the door latch and found the locking mechanism jammed with a molded compound. "Do any of you have firsthand experience with C4?" he asked.

Abby, Billy, and Marc chorused, "I do," but it was Abby who was closest and moved in to sniff the product.

"It's dime store modeling clay. Crooks use it all the time." Abby pulled out the twine and waved it in the air, moving the smoke away with her hand at the same time. "She didn't even try to match the color of fuse cording, and there's no detonator device attached. Just find something to dig the clay out of the latch with, and we're good to go."

Marc and Arlie flipped open their Leatherman tools at the same time as Billy pulled out his Swiss Army knife, digging his fingernail into the mechanism to choose which blade to use. "I gotta get me one of those," he said, then moved back to let one of the other two men clean out the lock.

"No worries," Marc said. "Arlie and I always have spares. We'll set you up, but just remember not to put it in your carryon bag. TSA confiscates barrels of these every year."

"And there you have it," Arlie said, opening the door. "Mac, you and Abby come over here where the air is clearer, but don't follow us. I have the feeling that the cane she pointed at Abby had more than a pointy stick incorporated in it."

Chapter 10
More than a cane

Some kinds of walking stick may be used by people with disabilities as a crutch. The walking stick has also historically been known to be used as a defensive or offensive weapon, and may conceal a knife or sword as in a swordstick.
https://en.wikipedia.org/wiki/Walking_stick

"Louie! His signal! It's gone! Just poof! Arlie's disappeared!"

Louie leaned over Charlene's shoulder. "So that's what it looks like. I didn't know for sure what you were babbling about, but I never saw an app like that. Is that why the ambulance got there so fast for Arlie when he got stabbed?"

"Yes, but Abby said it showed his vitals at near-death levels that night. Now they're gone!" Charlene realized she had been chewing on her index fingernail, but no longer cared. "My husband has disappeared, and I didn't even get to tell him the good news!"

"So, I was right? Maybe you do have three sons..." Louie asked, then put his hand on her arm again. "Calm down. If he was dead or injured, you'd still see his vital signs, even if they were flatlining. Remember, he's in the airport maintenance department and there are all sorts of electrical interferences in there. He's probably in a dead zone."

Gasp!

"He's *not* dead. It's just his little tracer can't send out signals. That also means he can't receive phone calls. And…"

"Yes. And, and…" Charlene prompted.

"Hold on. That's G on the other side of the parking lot, walking away from that beater Chrysler. Ten to one says it isn't hers and she stole it. Probably looked pretty good before she got her hands on it. Papa said she never could drive worth a lick and that's why she always had a chauffeur."

Charlene leaned across Louie's chest and watched the fur-swaddled old woman stab her cane into the ice and snow-covered parking lot toward the front door. "Look at that! She's opened the security door. She must have stolen a key."

"Yeah," Louie chuckled, "and she propped it open with the can of salt so she could get out easier. That works for me. Stay here. I'll be right back."

"Oh, no, no, no you don't," Charlene argued. "I'm coming

with you or you're staying here with me."

"Hmph. Okay. I'm staying here with you," Louie said. *Because if I don't, you'd follow me no matter what I said, and Arlie would kill me if I let anything happen to you.*

"You agreed a little too quickly for someone who was ready to act irrationally to get out to warn Arlie and Marc about her cane."

"And her blind side," Louie added. "I still want to do that, but I think I can be of more use out here right now. You're welcome to help me, unless you're afraid of knives." Louie pulled a switchblade out of his hip pocket and flicked it open, startling her.

He grinned at her reaction, the one he was hoping for. "The way I figure it, there are three seasoned cops—or two cops and a deputy marshal—in there and one little old lady. Unless G decided to start packing a semi-automatic weapon, she won't be able to do them all in. She only has two shots with that cane, and they're small caliber at that. If she hurts either the kid or the woman—Abby, right? —it'll make the men so mad, they'll knock her down at any cost. So, rational thinking says she'll go in, get the pin back or whatever it is she wants, and then she'll lock them in a bathroom or an office, then come back to her car and split."

He looked from the front door G was headed toward and subconsciously started counting. *Rookie mistake, parking so far away. As crippled up as she is, it's going to take her a long time to reach her getaway car. Anything can happen in the minute and a half it takes her to get behind that steering wheel.*

Louie looked over at Charlene and grinned. "Looks like it's time for me to puncture a couple of tires," then opened the door to leave.

"Make sure you only punch the tires on the passenger side so she won't see them when she gets back," Charlene said as he stepped out into the brisk and breezy cold.

He popped his head back in. "What? You think I was born yesterday?"

"I guess not," she mumbled, then turned up the heater and bent back to her smartphone screen, hoping his vitals signal would pop up again. "Maybe I can pull up the layout of the maintenance department and find out where the bathrooms and offices are. At least, it will give me something to do."

Two minutes later, Louie was back. "Pull up to a parking spot near the front door, but off to the left side so she won't see us." *I may not be able to avenge Papa's killing, but I can certainly have a front row seat when she gets popped!*

***

Damned! I should have parked closer to the front door!

"Argh! You bitch!" Charlene jumped out of her car and ran towards G for a tackle, and hopefully a face-pummeling.

Louie scrambled out after her and quickly overtook her. He pulled Charlene close, his hand over her mouth, swinging her away from the startled hag who already had her cane raised, ready to put a bullet in her would-be assailant.

"Sorry, sorry!" Louie called out to G over his shoulder, his back to Charlene's would-be victim. "My sister's crazy when it comes to fur coats."

He yelped as Charlene bit his hand but managed to keep it over her mouth. "She, um, got tangled up with some PETA nuts a while back and they...Ouch! Brainwashed her. It's your right to wear fur..."

"Hmph!" G grunted and lowered her cane, using it to hobble faster to her car. *Dumb fox hugger!*

"What are you trying to do," Louie whispered into Charlene's ear. "Get us both killed?"

Charlene huffed and shook her head, trying to get Louie's

120

hand off her mouth, but didn't try to bite him again.

"Are you ready to be quiet and act maybe just a little bit sane?" he asked.

She nodded, so he dropped his hand and relaxed his hold. "Look at her," Louie whispered. "She's pathetic. A broken-down car, a body that's in even worse shape, an evil personality, and two bullets in a modified cane to take on the world. She's not going far…"

Charlene snorted, then whispered hoarsely, "A murderess who scalps innocents, a thief, a conniver who has figured out how to escape a maximum-security prison, a heartless lump of flesh who intimidates little boys… She's a bitch in anyone's book and needs to be contained before she hurts anyone else."

The front door flew open, kicked free by Arlie's boot, the two cops and deputy streaming out, guns poised, ready for anything.

Or so they thought.

Arlie did a quick double-take, gawking at Louie's arms loosening their hold around Charlene. Marc quickly recognized her and said, "I got this, Arlie. Go take care of your wife."

Billy piped in, "I'll go back and get Abby and Mac, then," and turned around to go back into the building.

"Watch out for a ringer!" Louie called out to Marc.

"What?" Arlie asked, pulling Charlene close.

"Just in case she called in some back up," Louie said. "We didn't see anyone, but that Midwest muscle seems to pop in..."

Ping!

Ping! Ping!

"Are you okay?" Arlie asked, then saw the red blotch in Louie's right shoulder grow.

"I guess not," Louie mumbled, then slumped forward and groaned.

"I got him," Charlene said. "Go get the bastards."

Louie's eyes fluttered, then his head popped up. "I guess he's dyslexic, he shot me on the wrong side," then he stifled a laugh. "Call Billy and tell him to stay inside."

"Too late," Billy said, rushing over to squat down beside Louie and Charlene, huddled behind the concrete trash can receptacle. "Help me drag him inside. Abby's great with first aid."

Billy grunted as he tugged Louie by his arm pits toward the

door Charlene held open. "Damn! You're heavier than you look."

"I'm all muscle," Louie said, then started coughing again. "I guess I'd better shut up."

"Yeah, well, if you think of something important, don't keep it to yourself," Charlene said, coming around toward his head to help bring him into the foyer the rest of the way. "Just whisper it, and I'll do the hollering."

Billy raised his hand and said, "Hold on a sec."

The only sound was Louie stifling a cough.

"I don't hear anything," Charlene whispered.

Billy nodded his head, agreeing with her, his finger to his lips to tell her to stay mum.

"Did I get her?" An unfamiliar voice called out from the parking lot.

Arlie called back, "She won't be texting anyone for a while—you got both her hands—but she's not dead. Who are you?"

"Just put her back in prison where she belongs. Death is too good for her. Tell her it's a thank you from her youngest. Thanks for nothing!"

"Slinky," Louie whispered.

Billy looked at everyone, making sure they were safe, and called out to the parking lot. "We could use a little help in here."

"Why'd you say that?" Abby asked. "I got this. The bullet went right through."

"Slinky's a sharpshooter," Billy said. "He could have killed Louie and G if he wanted to. Sounds like he was just giving us a hand in putting her back in prison. He's a bit of a local legend, a vigilante in the backwoods of North Carolina. He's never killed anyone but does put the scare on some of the gangs when they get out of hand. No one's ever pressed charges, and I seriously doubt G will, either. You're not going to, are you, Louie?"

"I got shot by Slinky?" Louie glanced down at Abby's hands, applying pressure to both sides of the bullet hole on his right shoulder. "Cheaper and sexier than a tattoo! Nah, let him go. It's not worth the paperwork to bust him for discharging a firearm in the city, I'm sure. Glad to see he could get at least a little payback."

Louie's eyes dimmed. "But I wonder if he knows she probably killed Papa."

"Well, it doesn't make a difference to us right now, does

it?" Abby said. "Don't worry about tomorrow's problems. You have enough to deal with for today."

Chapter 11
To Say I Love You

How to Win Friends and Influence People is a self-help book written by Dale Carnegie, published in 1936. Over 30 million copies have been sold world-wide, making it one of the best-selling books of all time. In 2011, it was number 19 on Time Magazine's list of the 100 most influential books. (https://en.wikipedia.org/wiki/How_to_Win_Friends_and_Influence_People)

"You seem so laid back about getting shot, Louie," Charlene said, offering him a sip of his whipped cream and chocolate shavings-topped hot cocoa.

"Yeah, well, I think Slinky may have recognized me. If that's the case, I guess I'd better get out of town. If he figured it out, then someone else might have, too. I suppose I'm not as clever as I thought."

"That still doesn't tell me why it doesn't bother you that someone shot you."

"Well, I sorta, kinda shot him first. I was just a kid. He was my crippled uncle and I used to pester him. He was confined to a wheelchair and the other kids and I would run up on him and poke him with a stick or throw a ball at him. Not a soft foam ball, either. One day, I shot him with a pellet gun. Just in the shoulder. I didn't put out an eye or anything. Anyhow, he used to say, 'I'll get you when you're not looking, when you least expect it.'"

Louie shifted positions and sat up straighter. "I told him, 'Go ahead and see if I care.'" He started to laugh, then coughed with discomfort and settled for a quick chuckle. "I guess I really don't care. I deserved it. He was smart and got away from the family business as soon as he was of legal age. Because of his disability—I think it was spina bifida or something that sounded like that—Papa didn't send him to the same schools as Alonzo and my Uncle Luca. He had a private tutor. She was Swiss or Dutch, I think. I remember thinking how pretty she was, but maybe that was because she had blond hair and everyone else in the household had black hair. Even me, of course, because Ma kept me colored with Lady Clairol when we went to visit Papa. Yeah, I think Slinky's tutor rescued him from having to be part of Papa's evil lifestyle."

"How's the ornery patient?" Arlie asked as he stepped

inside the hospital room, bringing up the suddenly glum atmosphere with a tone of jest.

"I'm still breathing out of all the right holes. No hissing or leaking out of the extra ones."

"Just dropped in to check on you and tell you they've carted G away, both hands bound up like she was getting ready to box the Abominable Snowman. They were able to retrieve her smart tablet for me but couldn't find the teddy bear pin. She must have dropped it on the way to the car or something." Arlie sighed in feigned exasperation. "Oh, well. I guess I'll have to develop my own little spybot."

Marc followed behind him. "Hey, Louie! I brought you something: a book," and handed Louie a brown paper-wrapped package. "You do know how to read, don't you?" he asked and added a wink of mischief.

"Just shows you how much you don't know about me. I'm a voracious reader. I progressed beyond picture books two whole years ago." Louie laughed at his own joke, then peeled back the wrapping paper. "'How to Win Friends and Influence People?' Really, Marc? Hmm. Maybe I should write a gangster exposé. Let folks know how easily the bad guys influence decent people the wrong way every day."

"The doctor said he can leave any time he wants," Charlene told Arlie, "but not to do any heavy lifting. Nothing more than the remote control or a piece of pizza. Oh, and I volunteered to pop in on him every day and change his dressings. It's the least I can do. He saved our lives."

"He what?" Marc and Arlie asked.

"Knock, knock," Billy said, then peeked into the hospital room. "Can you fit two more in here?"

"Yeah, because we brought you a present," Mac said, lifting the colorful gift bag to Louie.

Louie set his half-unwrapped book down, took the bag, and started pulling out the bright tissue paper packing material. "A teddy bear? Really? A real teddy bear?" Louie hugged the caramel-colored stuffed animal, and said, "This is so awesome! Believe it or not, this is my first teddy bear." He hugged it again. "Can I name him Mac? I'll never forget you or the bear, but Mac is such a magical name."

"If you push his right paw, he plays a lullaby. His feet are ticklish, so if you push them, he giggles," Mac said, coming close to show him.

"What happens if I squeeze his left paw?" Louie asked, his fingers poised, ready to push.

"Try it," Mac said, and giggled into his hand.

'I love you sooo much.'

Tears welled in Louie's eyes. "I love you, too," he said and squeezed his teddy bear, wiping his tears in the plush animal's fur. "I think every person needs to say that at least once a year to someone."

"Oh, and Arlie," Mac said, and turned to look up at him. "I, um, did a bit of a magic trick when I put the teddy bear pin into the inside-out piggy bank." Mac reached in his jacket pocket and produced a wad of toilet paper. "I thought you might want to keep the teddy bear pin and take it apart to see how it worked."

Mac giggled into his hand after Arlie took the bundle from him. "I put the little troll doll that Carlos won for me at the claw machine game into the box. I'll bet she was mad when she found it. Oh, and I wrapped it up for you, so the sharp end didn't poke you. Don't worry—the toilet paper's clean."

"Well, thanks, Mac. That was quick thinking on your part. You've saved me a lot of trouble."

"That's my boy, practicing the sleight-of-hand tricks Grandpa taught him on the unsuspecting," Billy said. "By the way, Louie, it's up to you what you do with this information, but I got a text referencing you just a few minutes ago. It was relayed to me by one of my North Carolina contacts. 'Tell the kid she won't be bothering him again and that his new secret home is safe with me,' and was signed Uncle S."

"So, I won't have to leave Alaska if I don't want to? Slinky's not going to let anyone know where I am?" Louie asked.

"Why would he?" Charlene asked. "It doesn't seem like he's too fond of her or any of those creeps."

Arlie patted her on the shoulder then cleared his voice. "I hate to interfere with your magical moment, Louie, but what did you mean, dear wife, when you said that Louie saved your lives?"

"He doesn't know?" Louie asked, a grin blossoming on his tear-streaked face.

"Know what?" Arlie asked, looking back and forth between Louie and Charlene.

"Well, um," Charlene stalled, "You know how I've been a little more, shall we say 'impetuous' lately?"

"You mean like shipping the kids off to a friend's house, so you can tail me into a dangerous situation? And attacking a known murderess with only your bare hands?" Arlie asked, eyes squinted in admonition.

"Yeah, well, I guess I've been a little extra hormonal lately. It happened when I was pregnant with Chip, too. By that time, I realized my fiancé was a jerk and I had moved back in with my dad. He said it was a good thing he was my father and loved me so much because a newlywed husband might not put up with the crazies I was going through."

"Well, letting me know what's going on is the most important part of dealing with the changes that are happening with your moods and your body. It's going to be a completely different experience this time, dear. You have a loving husband and two young boys looking out for you and our new little one."

"Plus," Louie said, still excited that he didn't have to leave Alaska, "you have me now, too! I always wanted to be an uncle."

Arlie came around and put his arm over Louie's good shoulder. "Thanks, bud, for taking care of her even if she wasn't your responsibility. You saved my life a couple months ago, and yesterday looked out for my wife and our wee one, too. You may have done it out of the goodness of your heart, but it also earned you the right to be her brother and therefore, the uncle to our boys."

"Or the boys and their sister," Charlene said. "I still think we're having a daughter."

"Or one of each," Billy added. "Life is full of surprises." He looked at Mac and smiled. "Believe me, I know."

THE END

A Note from the Author

Thank you for reading ALWAYS A BIGGER FISH, the third book in the ARLIE UNDERCOVER series. This book is unique in that it melds three of my book series: ARLIE UNDERCOVER, THE FAIRIES SAGA, and BENJI, THE LOST YEARS.

If you'd like to know more about Billy Burke—and find out more about his sarcastic inner reflection on cousins in the 18th century—check out AYE, I AM A FAIRY and THE GREAT BIG FAIRY (where we first meet Mac). How did G wind up in prison? That's in POOL BOY WANTED: NO EXPERIENCE PREFERRED, a rather randy novella that is also part of the box set UNFORGETTABLE SUSPENSE.

Authors love reviews!

If you enjoyed this story, I would appreciate it if you'd help others know a bit about it, too. Others will find your reading experience helpful when deciding if this is a book for them.
Please leave a review on Amazon and/or Goodreads.
If you're interested in the other books or projects I'm working on, please sign up for Time Travelers Anonymous (my newsletter) at **http://bit.ly/DaniHaviland**
and follow me on BookBub. **http://bit.ly/BBDani**
and Goodreads **http://bit.ly/2DHgdrds**

Thank you!

Other books by Dani Haviland

A Stingray Christmas: (First book in the Arlie Undercover series) Anchorage detective on medical leave travels from Alaska to Arizona to see for the first time the son he'd fathered as an anonymous sperm donor. Great and rotten surprises await the cop with the smartest smartphone around.

The Biggest Heart Ever: (Book two in the Arlie Undercover series) When would Arlie learn that trying to do everything by himself could be deadly—and make Charlene a widow before they were married?

CONTEMPORARY NOVELLAS – BENJI, THE LOST YEARS (Benji is young Mac's godfather/biological father and has some very interesting events occur in his time traveling life)

Luke the Unexpected: Love of classic motorcycles brought them together, but Luke and Holly have other challenges to face. Find out how their friend Benji got his stripes here.

Pool Boy Wanted: No Experience Preferred (rather racy) Young Benji has been a hostage and slave, but life gets worse when an older woman decides she wants him as her own.

THE FAIRIES SAGA SERIES (in order with novellas):

Naked in the Winter Wind: (lengthy novel) How does an older woman wind up as a young hottie in Revolutionary War era North Carolina? First book in the time travel series.

Ha'Penny Jenny: (historical novella) More about the naïve and psychic young girl who was adopted into a time traveling family. Will her past catch up to her?

Aye, I am a Fairy: (lengthy novel) Young British lord finds himself entwined with a time traveling family and must decide if he should go back in time, too. Second book in the series.

Dances Naked: (novel) Directionally challenged time traveler Marty Melbourne is rescued by Cherokee in 18th century. What must he do before the chief will show him to The Trees, the portal through time?

Chasing Christmas: (historical novella) A young Cherokee is rescued from an abusive man and changes the lives of many in this 18th century America family.

The Great Big Fairy: (lengthy novel) Very tall Benji grew up in the 20th century but was born in the 18th. When he finds a way to return to his grandparents in the distant past, he goes for it. Once there, he realizes he can't stay, but must return to the future. Fourth book in the series.

Little Bear and the Ladies: (historical novella) What's a bachelor trapper to do with all the females he rescues from the Hessian mercenaries? He'd better hurry and figure something!

Little Drummer Boy: (historical novella) Young Scout works to earn money for a home in post-Revolutionary War America but runs up against prejudices and snowstorms.

Never Too Young: (historical novella) Scout and Ha'Penny Jenny have grown up, but will they be able to spend their life together, or will the past and ruffians get in their way?

Time in a Little Blue Bottle: Mark Twain, Elvis, the prime vampire Cleveland, and time traveler Marty Melbourne help two youths thwart the bad guys who are out to steal Fountain of Youth water.

STAND ALONE NOVELLAS

Kit Kringle: An Alaskan Tale (contemporary) Kay moved to Alaska for the wrong reasons, then decided to stay and start her own business. What she hadn't planned on were prejudices and falling in love.

Be My Angel: (contemporary) The love of horses brought them together. Could a greedy woman break them apart?

Three Are One: (contemporary) A wounded warrior from another perspective: the widow and child left behind to deal with the soldier's suicide. Could Heath heal them?

One Arctic Summer (contemporary) The touch she never forgot.

Dani Haviland has never been one to believe, "You can't do that!" She started her own business in 1994, selling tractor parts in Alaska, then segued to writing and publishing books, becoming a *USA Today* bestselling author in the process.

Always full of optimism and a grateful attitude, she finds humor or opportunity – or both – in even the most horrid fictional circumstances, then helps her characters overcome them. How? Read and find out.

She currently splits her time between Alaska and Oregon, tirelessly writing and gardening, publishing and promoting, while claiming to be 'retired.'

Contact

Dani Haviland can be found at:

Amazon Author page: http://bit.ly/dhAuthor

Newsletter sign up: http://bit.ly/2DHnews

Website: http://bit.ly/DaniHaviland

Twitter: @dani_haviland

Facebook: https://www.facebook.com/dani.haviland (or

search Dani Haviland Author)

BookBub: http://bit.ly/BBDani

Email: dani@danihaviland.com